CONFINED DESIRES

KATHERINE MCINTYRE

HOT TREE PUBLISHING

For information, contact the publisher, Hot Tree Publishing.

www.hottreepublishing.com

Editing: Hot Tree Editing

Cover Designer: BookSmith Design

E-book ISBN: 978-1-922359-64-3

Paperback ISBN: 978-1-922359-65-0

To everyone who struggled through the pandemic--may you find silver linings amidst hardship.

CHAPTER ONE

SKY STRODE INTO HER KITCHEN, CAREFUL NOT TO CREAK along the linoleum. She wasn't used to sneaking around her apartment and tended to march around like an elephant with steel-dipped soles, but she didn't want to disturb her guest.

Mia had arrived yesterday, late enough that even a night owl like her was ready to pass the hell out. They'd barely gotten a chance to chat before Sky set up the futon for her and then they both crashed. Which left about a thousand questions swirling through her mind, ones that wouldn't exist if Sky had sent more than the occasional email or text over the past five years.

They'd been high school besties who'd dropped off the map when Mia went to college across the country in Seattle, and Sky stayed at home going to culinary school instead. Tale as old as the stale crackers in the back of her pantry.

Byron and Shelley perked at the sound of her moving around, but before the obnoxious meowls could begin, she poured out kibble into their little metal dishes. Her two tabbies rushed for the bowls and dunked their greedy heads in. Clearly, she starved them.

Sky set about to assembling her coffee for the day, strong enough to kick her teeth in. Normally, she finished the twelve-cup carafe by her lonesome, but she supposed she could share a drop or two. As she set the grounds in the gold cone filter, her gaze drifted over to where Mia lay on the futon fast asleep.

The woman had curled to her side. The purple down comforter tangled between her legs, revealing her creamy, toned thighs in the miniscule Kelly green shorts she wore. Her rich brown hair cascaded in a tumble of waves, and with her eyes closed, she looked so gorgeous Sky's breath caught in her throat.

After years of crushing on this woman, she should've gotten over those fantasies by now. When Mia lived a billion miles away in Seattle, she could try to forget. But when she was here? In her house? The urge to go over and sniff Mia's glossy locks surged strong, but Sky wasn't a total creep. Just an idiot for agreeing to let the newly single woman crash on her futon for the next few weeks. Time to play the game of how many hours of overtime could she cram in without making it seem like she was hardcore avoiding Mia.

The coffee maker sputtered as it set to the arduous task.

The sound caused Mia's lashes to flutter, and a moment later, a groan came from the futon as she stretched her arms overhead. Sky stared at the thin line of coffee filling into the carafe. So much for slipping out undetected. The creak of footsteps sounded, and Sky looked up to see Mia approaching in a loose gray tank top, no bra, and shorts that may as well have been underwear. Not like she could complain about the stunning view, but Christ, the sight made tamping down her libido even harder.

Mia let out a yawn and wiped the sleep from her eyes as she settled by Sky's side. Sky ran a hand through her finger-length hair, recently shorn, trying to avoid the prickling heat that crawled up her neck.

"Are you making coffee?" Mia asked. "God, I love you. I could drink a gallon after how late I got in last night."

Well, the blush took the cue and spread everywhere. A few weeks. She'd lock herself to her sous station, and they'd have minimal exchanges through the whole stay. All above board and friendly-like. She could handle this.

"Yeah, let me grab the cups," she said, her voice coming out gruffer than intended. She rattled around in her cupboard, pulling out the "cats and caffeine" mug as well as the big red one she loved. "Do you have to work this morning, or do you get a chance to settle in?"

"Not working until tomorrow, thankfully," Mia said, leaning against the countertop. "What about you? You work at a fancy restaurant now, right?"

"Lumiere," Sky said, "Right on the Waterfront." She brought the mugs over to the machine, which chugged out the final drops of coffee into the carafe. The place she worked now was a dream job—far different from the rinky-dink diners and burger joints she first slaved away at until she packed some print onto her résumé. She poured the two steaming cups of coffee and set out cream and sugar, letting Mia do her thing.

"Damn, girl. Look at you rocking the restaurant world." Mia nudged her in the side. She picked up one of the cups, doused it in cream, and lifted the piping hot liquid to her lips. Mia's blue eyes grew a little more serious as she locked gazes with Sky. Not like

Sky could look away if she wanted—the woman had spellbinding deep blues, like stepping to the edge of the beach to stare out at the ocean.

"Sky, I've been a shit friend," Mia said, her voice lowering a pitch. "I got so wrapped up in college and then Derek that I never checked in on you or anything. And I know I'm back home, showing up here like no time's passed, but I wanted to say I fucked up. When I thought about who to reach out to about the big life change, you were the first person who popped into my head. That means something."

Of course this woman would dive deep the first chance she got.

Sky's cheeks colored, and she took a sip of her black coffee. "Hey, Mia B, communication's a two-way street. I got so consumed in the chef life, which means working way too many hours, and I dropped off too."

She didn't mention the fact that her avoidance had been a little more on purpose. Unrequited love was a punishment she wouldn't inflict on anyone.

"Let's make a pact," Mia said, thrusting out her pinky finger. "We'll make the effort this time to keep in contact. You're too important to me, and I don't want to make that mistake again."

"You've always meant the world to me, Mia B," Sky murmured, unable to keep the scrape of vulnerability from her voice as she lifted her pinky finger and entwined it around Mia's. "I promise."

Even if that meant she'd need to get into the dating scene ASAP, reactivate Tinder, whatever. Anything to push these feelings into the battered box they belonged. No amount of logic would suppress the way her heart thumped and her chest diesel-engine roared. Two weeks in her place. She could survive this.

With a blink, Sky realized their pinkies were still entwined, and Mia stared at her with a curious gleam in her eyes. Sky snatched her hand back and ran her fingers through her hair.

"So, is your mom thrilled you're home?" Sky asked. She was curious as to the whole breakup too, but she didn't want to drag Mia over broken glass right now.

Mia shrugged. "Kind of? She's excited to see me, but her new boyfriend ranks higher on the concern list as per usual. Hence why I couldn't crash there."

Irritation prickled under Sky's skin. "That's fucked. You're her daughter and should absolutely come first."

Mia twined her arms around Sky and leaned her head against her shoulder. "See, this is why I missed you so damn much."

Sky froze, unable to move. Part of her melted at this touch, while the other freaked out. The last thing Mia needed was her best friend dumping a lifelong crush on her lap. This close, she could feel the woman's sleepy heat, and the sweet scent of peaches wafted off her. Sky's mouth watered—the response instinctual. She forced her hand up to run her fingers through Mia's silken strands. That was friendly, right?

"Missed you too, babe," she murmured.

"So, wait, are you working tonight, or no?" Mia asked, pulling away to grab her mug.

"Uh, no," Sky murmured, mind racing as she tried to come up with an excuse to leave.

Mia tapped the edge of her mug with her fingernail. "Then maybe we could take the day to play catch up?" she asked. When Sky didn't respond, the words refusing to leave her tongue, Mia's eyes widened. "I mean, as long as you didn't have plans or anything. I know I kind of dropped this on you. Fuck, I don't even know if you're seeing anyone or who you hang out with anymore."

"Pitifully single," Sky responded. "My girlfriend and I split up last year, and I've been so busy with work that I haven't been able to get out to the bars or clubs in Philly at all to jump back into the dating scene. Trust me, you haven't missed much."

"Bullshit," Mia said, placing her mug of coffee down. "Get dressed. We're heading out to Lucky's, and I'm buying you breakfast." Her blue eyes twinkled as she doled out the commands, and Sky's heart thumped harder.

Sky scratched the nape of her neck. "Yes, ma'am."

She headed to the bedroom, cursing her lack of an excuse. A large part of her was thrilled to be spending all of this time around Mia after so long. Yet the other part of her just wanted to solder metal sheets around her heart.

As if she'd stand a chance with Mia Brownstone living at her house for the next two weeks.

***

"DID YOU REALLY ORDER AVOCADO TOAST?" MIA ASKED from across the table—her plate piled high with bacon and blueberry pancakes.

Sky flipped her the middle finger. "Don't knock this perfection until you've tried it. Lucky's makes the best damn avocado toast around here." She took a big bite for emphasis, enjoying the sea salt, avocado, and brioche combo as the flavors exploded on her tongue.

"God, you are a different person," Mia responded, a mischievous glint in her eyes. That was one of the things Sky loved best about her in high school, the wicked lightness when Mia would get some spark of an adventure or crazy impulse they had to follow. And hell, Sky had been so puppy-dog smitten, she would've followed her anywhere. Which she had—to more abandoned buildings and weird trails in random parks than she could count.

A news alert buzzed on her phone again. More on the damn virus sweeping the globe. She tried to tune the chatter out with loud music at work and shutting off the news at home, but it infiltrated any way possible.

"This TELA flu has been infecting everything," Sky mumbled. A slight jitter buzzed beneath her skin at the thought of it, but honestly, she'd just been trying to tamp down those anxieties.

"Hopefully not us," Mia said, taking a swig from her orange juice. "Back in Seattle, they started to make some precautionary closures. More cases were cropping up, and folks were starting to die."

Sky made an X symbol with her fingers. "Better keep your plague away from me, babe."

Mia's grin was impish. "I'm pretty sure I slumped all over you enough that you're fucked, but I can up the ante." She reached out and gripped Sky's hand in hers. "Look at that. Plague-ridden."

Sky rolled her eyes, but she didn't make any motion to tug her hand away. She'd be lying if she said this wasn't everything she'd imagined for years—

sitting in a diner with Mia and holding hands. Her palm began to sweat and everything, but whatever. She'd take these moments and then clutch them tight to her chest on all the nights her starchy sheets were freezing, and Byron and Shelley cuddled with each other and not her.

Sky pulled her hand away first to take another bite of her breakfast, before her mind reeled with any more fanciful ideas. Besides, Mia's hands were all dainty and soft. Sky had chef hands—covered with slight scars, burns, and calluses. Even still, she didn't miss how Mia's gaze lingered.

The air felt charged between them, as if words hovered on the tip of Mia's tongue too, not just the thousands that Sky had swallowed back over the years. Sky forced herself to look away.

"So, I know you're the IT queen now and all, but please tell me you're getting some painting done," Sky said, breaking the tension that remained.

Mia's lips curled into a Cheshire grin. "At least a little bit. If I didn't get my aggression out on canvas, I'd go on a rampage."

"They'd have to turn you on and off again," Sky teased.

Mia rolled her eyes. "Clever. I've never heard that

phrase in my life. Don't tell me your day-to-day's been nothing but work since we last saw each other."

"I mean, I also have a pair of cats. You may have met them. And my voluminous collection of romance novels is keeping me warm at night." Sky chewed on the remainder of her avocado toast, trying to ignore the blanket of lameness that coated her shoulders. Sure, she hiked sometimes, met up with her friends for bar nights at Renegades, and serenaded her staff to sous-chef karaoke when the pressure got too bad, but she loved where she worked and what she did.

Mia finished off her orange juice. "Well, I'm planning on staying in the area for a while, so you'd better get ready for some impromptu adventures. There are about a thousand abandoned buildings we haven't explored yet."

"You mean you've finally lived down the time you ran through the woods for fifteen straight minutes because you swore the squirrel was a cop?" Sky teased. "Because it was definitely a squirrel. Little bushy tail, beady eyes, and all."

"You're full of shit, Jenkins," Mia shot back. "It was a cop, and you just weren't paying attention."

"Clearly, the squirrel carried a small service revolver and a nightstick, which is why you ran like you'd been caught streaking." She couldn't help the sarcasm that dripped from her lips, but the cops and squirrel debate had gotten raised at least once a month through the rest of their time in high school. As much as she'd been worried about things being awkward since they hadn't talked for five years, both of them vaulted back like no time passed.

Fuck, she needed to find some way to get this crush out of her system, because this friendship had been so damn important to her.

She couldn't lose Mia again.

CHAPTER TWO

MIA PUSHED THE BROWNING MEAT AROUND ON THE skillet, the steam carrying the rich scents of the cumin, paprika, and chili powder she'd added. Might not be Michelin Five Star cooking like Sky could do, but she figured stocking up her bestie's fridge and cooking her dinner might place a dent in the massive debt she owed her. Plus, who could fuck up tacos?

After all, until Derek dumped her and half of their friends started ghosting her texts, she hadn't realized how few people she could still rely on. The first person who'd popped up in her mind at the idea of moving home was Skylar Jenkins, the woman she'd spent almost every day with from half of grade school into high school.

She glanced at Sky, who hunkered down on the

futon, attempting to read her contemporary romance. Not like Mia missed the way she fidgeted or hadn't turned a page in a while. Sky was an avid reader, but she obviously had trouble sitting still while Mia worked in her kitchen. Too bad. Sky was the best person she knew and the only one she could've counted on for a safe place to crash down when her life turned into an airplane wreck.

Her best friend had somehow gotten hotter in their time apart. With her long, muscular limbs, her scarred hands, and thick brown hair cut into a side-shave, Mia found it shocking the woman wasn't seeing anyone. Sky's dark penetrating eyes were her favorite feature though—they'd always made her feel seen. Truth be told, Sky had always made her heart accelerate the moment she stepped into the room, but Mia hadn't figured out her bisexual side until college.

The meat sizzled, drawing her attention front and center. She'd already cooked up beans and rice, which sat on the other stovetop. "All right, dinner's almost done," Mia called over. "You can quit pretending to read and come grab plates."

Sky snorted and hopped up from the futon, popping her book onto the arm. She strode over with a bit of a swagger that accentuated her full hips, and Mia tried not to lick her lips in response. She and

Derek broke up two months ago, but her libido raced in overdrive. Even before they'd split, the usual signs were there—dwindling sex life, barely any touch, and an increasing number of fights.

"I'll have you know I managed a full two and a half pages while you were cooking," Sky said, leaning beside her to take a sniff of the taco meat. "Good job, babe. You didn't burn down the kitchen this time."

A laugh exploded from her throat. "One time. One time when I was sixteen, you asshole!"

"One time is significant when setting fires to the kitchen," Sky commented, drawing plates from her cupboards with a clink. "I've never done it."

Cocky bastard. Mia couldn't help her grin. While the rest of the house contained stacks of books piled haphazardly, sweaters draped on the arms of couches, and a myriad assortment of pens and crumpled papers on almost every available surface, the kitchen was the opposite. Everything was neat, meticulous, and labeled, making it clear the woman worked as a chef.

Mia cracked open the box of taco shells and passed them over. "How are you going to have room for dinner with the size of your ego? Come on, let's dig in." She loaded up her taco shells with the usual suspects, more than a little nervous about Sky eating her cooking. She'd gotten marginally better in the kitchen, but she'd still only mastered a few recipes.

Sky assembled her own tacos with a swiftness that seemed habit—probably from working the line. Then she tilted her head toward the couch in her living room, visible from an open floorplan separated by the breakfast nook. Sky's apartment wasn't massive, but Mia loved how the sun streamed in through the wide windows, causing the peach walls to glow.

"We can eat in here or over on the couches if you like," Sky said. "I usually eat on the couches and fend off the cats. But I understand if you're used to eating like a civilized adult."

Mia couldn't hide her grin. Being here for a single day, she'd smiled more than she had in half a year. "Let's be real, I'll eat off the floor if I need to."

"I wouldn't advise that," Sky warned as she wove her way over to the couch opposite the futon Mia had slept on. "With Byron and Shelley on the prowl, you need any extra high ground you can get."

Mia snorted. The cats were new additions, but the lit geekery wasn't. They'd spent so many quiet after-noons out at Brandywine Park—Sky buried in a book while Mia sketched away. Sky popped onto the couch right in the middle, but Mia didn't want to eat all the way across the room from her. She stepped beside her and sank into the cushions, close enough their legs brushed. The simple touch was static electricity, a shock of awareness she wasn't used to.

Sky had always been comfortable. Safe. But in the time apart, something in their relationship shifted.

Mia took the first bite of sour cream, ground beef, and cheese, the explosion of salt and fat hitting her tongue just right. All too fast, the taco broke and things got messier than planned. She tried to lick the dollop of sour cream off the corner of her mouth, but Sky's gaze had drifted her way. A hesitant grin broke out on her lips, even though something intense existed in the woman's gaze.

Mia's cheeks flushed. "Yes, I'm still a mess when I eat." This awareness hadn't existed between her and Sky before—she'd talked to her with smeared chocolate around her mouth without a care, but right now, self-consciousness flushed through her. She'd also been oblivious to just how hot she'd found her best friend through most of high school, and Sky had only gotten sexier.

Sky's grin widened. "My bad, I should've grabbed paper towels." She pushed up off the couch and snagged a roll from the counter, handing it over. "Don't use the whole thing in one go," she teased.

Mia rolled her eyes. Shelley and Byron snuck

forward, their small paws extending in a joint effort to rob her of her dinner. Mia yanked her plate out of the way before accepting the proffered paper towel and wiping her mouth down.

"So, fill me in on the big stuff, Sky," Mia said, anxious to throw some of the attention off of her. "Hopes and dreams? True loves and heartbreaks?"

Sky finished chewing another bite of taco, all too neatly, before she lifted her hands in the air. "Whoa, that sort of conversation requires a bottle of Jack and a little more foreplay at the very least."

Mia couldn't help the heat rising to her cheeks, so she dove back in for another bite of her food, making another mess of herself. At least this time she had a paper towel to clean up. She just wanted to dispel this tension that settled between them, something that hadn't buzzed there when they were teenagers who spent every day together.

When she finished wiping off her mouth, she caught Sky's gaze again, those serious eyes boring into her like she could strip her soul bare with turpentine. Her heart ached with how badly she needed to feel seen right now, how much she longed to be understood. Derek's parting phrase pretty much drove the last rusted nail in that he'd never understood her at all.

You're just desperate for someone to need you because

you don't want to be alone.

Sure, she'd bend over backward to help the people she cared about and often got way more involved than necessary, but the opposite was worse. Standing alone at the bar, in her room, at the park, looking out as everyone shared camaraderie and warmth except for her. After all, she'd seen how many guys left her mom, again and again and again. Maybe something in her genetic makeup just repulsed other people.

The only one who'd never made her feel that way was the woman sitting beside her.

Sky finished up her last taco and patted Mia on the knee. "Hey, if you bring the Jack, we'll see what we can do."

Mia's grin came unbidden, brighter than she thought possible. "Deal."

"Dinner was delicious," Sky called, heading over to begin putting away the rest of the food into Tupperware. "Thanks, Mia B."

Mia swallowed hard. The familiar nickname caused her chest to ache. From the second she stepped into Sky's apartment, she'd grown sure of one thing. Even if adjusting took her a little while, the move home was the right call.

MIA ARRIVED AT THE RIVERWALK WITH TWO CUPS OF Wawa coffee. She'd been desperate to get her hands on some from the moment she got home. Seattle might have a lot of spectacular coffee, but they didn't have a Wawa.

She walked down the pale planks of the small boardwalk, watching the sun glitter off the surface of the river. Even though they'd entered spring, the temp hadn't quite caught the memo yet, so she wore her winter jacket still. On one of the nearby benches was a familiar figure.

Mom leaned against the bench, her arms spread out on either side. Her mother had the same deep brown hair and blue eyes she did, but the similarities ended there. Mia had inherited her father's soft nose and his full lips, while her mother's sharper features always reminded her of a sparrow. Plus, she had a fair number of freckles and mid-toned skin, different from her mother's smooth olive skin.

Mom glanced her way and offered a big wave, but she didn't make a motion to get up. Mia walked over and plopped onto the bench beside her. She thrust out the extra coffee that she'd been using for a hand-warmer on her walk.

"Sweetheart, it's so good to see you," Mom said, snagging the coffee and wrapping an arm around her in a quick hug. As always, Mia fought the temptation to lean in more, to see if she could extend the hug at all, but Mom pulled back too fast. Carol Brownstone wasn't a hugger, not even with her boyfriends, which was the polar opposite of Mia, who needed touch like she needed coffee in the morning.

"Well, figured after a break-up like that, I could use a change of pace," Mia said. "Seattle was never mine anyway." For a little while, she thought the city might be. When Derek had gotten more serious and they'd moved in together after college, she believed she'd caught a glimpse of her future spanning out before her.

"Derek's loss," Mom said. "He was a bit of an asshole anyway."

Mia choked back the words leaping to her lips: *Like your last five boyfriends?* She doubted that would go over well with Mom. No matter how much they butted heads, Mia always reminded herself to be grateful. Her mom tried her best, even though they were so different, but the bitterness had corroded the woman more and more after Dad abandoned them to run off to the West Coast with his secret girlfriend.

"Yeah, probably better we didn't do the whole marriage and babies thing," Mia said. Her throat grew thick at the admission. She knew better than to slip with that.

Mom lifted an eyebrow, giving her an arched look. "You're better off pursuing a career than that nonsense."

Mia's hackles rose, the old familiar fights rising to the surface like a reflex. Mom tried so much to get her to choke down the same bitter brew, but it only made Mia the opposite. She fought for all of the things her mother told her to avoid for years, and honestly, a flicker of hope had existed with Derek. When they'd first started dating, he made her soup from scratch when she got sick, took late-night walks with her where they talked for hours, and gave her the lazy cuddles, hand-holding, and hugs she'd been craving for so long.

"I'll do what I do, Ma," she responded, taking a defensive sip of her coffee. The Irish cream coated her tongue like candy, the reassurance she needed right now.

"Good thing you moved now too," Mom said. She hadn't touched her coffee yet, staring out over the river. "The spread of the virus is getting worse and they're talking closures."

Mia shrugged. "Let's just hope I find an apartment before that. Can't crash on Sky's couch forever."

"How's Sky doing?" Mom asked. "You haven't mentioned her in years."

A flush stained her cheeks. She wasn't wrong, but it was a sore spot for Mia. She hated how wrapped up she'd gotten in college and her new life, how she'd discarded everyone from back home.

Almost like her father had.

Bile rose in her throat. "Sky's doing great,' she said, trying to distract herself. "She's working as a chef at Lumiere now. We should check out the restaurant sometime."

Mom let out a low whistle. "That place is way out of my paygrade, sweetheart. But good on her. She was always a hard worker."

"Yeah, she's great," Mia murmured in response, for once in agreement with her mother. Sky had always been the sort of loyal she'd always dreamed of, and even in their time apart, that hadn't changed. Mia wouldn't make the mistake of letting her go twice.

"We'll have to grab dinner sometime soon," Mom said, standing up from the bench.

Disappointment tugged at her heels, but she tried to suck in a breath and not let it filter too deep. Mom still hadn't touched her coffee. She pushed up from the bench, too, and opened her arms in an attempt for a hug. Her mother stepped in, patting her back lightly, and stepped out, as if they'd engaged in some minimal contact dance.

"Remember, sweetheart," Mom called out as she strolled past her, "find somewhere soon, before the virus shutdowns spread over here."

"Will do," she said, lifting her hand in a wave. Mia took another sip of her coffee before she sank onto the bench, the cool crisscross sinking in past her jeans. She didn't know what she'd been expecting—she knew her mother. But after the coldness from Derek, from her former friends, she desperately needed some sunlight in her life.

Wilmington's office buildings stretched high in the distance, framing the beautiful river in front of her. Even if most of her friendships as a kid wouldn't hold up, she still had Sky Jenkins, by some miracle. She could keep building from there, one step at a time. Starting over was never easy, but the fresh slate offered a chance to try.

Mia finished the last sip of her coffee, watching the mesmerizing glitter of the dappled sunbeams over the water. She pushed up from the bench and tossed her empty cup in the nearby trash can.

Mia sucked in a deep breath, staring at the planked walkway in front of her.

One step at a time.

CHAPTER THREE

After a week of Mia in her apartment, one thing grew certain.

Sky's crush on Mia Brownstone hadn't diminished at all. Instead, it doubled her investment, to the point she would need a new vibrator when all was said and done.

Which was why she was grateful to be at Lumiere right now, rather than ogling her temporary roommate. She chopped up more wild mushrooms for the coq au vin Bill prepared. Sizzles and clanks sounded around her, the chaotic melody of the kitchens one she adored. Greg slopped around at the dishwasher, suds flying in his wake, and Mateo stood next to her, chopping at the vegetables with blinding efficiency.

"Duck confit for table ten," Bill hollered, his voice

ringing through the place. He lined the dish up to the order station.

Cassidy swept out to grab the piping hot dish. "Got it," she called back sweetly. She offered a flirty wink to Sky as she passed, sashaying with a bit more swing to her hips.

"You're a goddamn tease, Cass," Sky called out, unaffected. The woman had a serious boyfriend but also happened to be a perennial flirt. Though if the woman was single and interested in women, that would be a whole different story. Then Sky would turn into a sputtering mess, because she melted into a puddle around anyone who might be interested in her.

The knife moved to the cutting board with a smooth liquidity, and she basked in the familiar chopping motion.

Mateo nudged her in the side. "You start stocking up? The grocery stores are insane right now."

Sky's brows drew together, even as she continued the constant movement of being back here, like a dance from the stations to the fridges. She grabbed the stock she'd pulled out over to the side and added the extra ingredients in the mix. She brought the liquid over to a pan and set it to simmer, prepping for Bill.

"What are you on about, Matty boy?" Sky asked,

not looking over his way as she stirred what would be the reduction.

"The first few cases of TELA broke in Philly, and folks are panicking," he said, whisking away at the batter for the dessert crepes he prepped. "They're talking about setting some lockdowns in place, things shutting down like they're doing overseas in Spain and Germany."

Liam swept in to grab the order for table six. "If I have to hear TELA talk back here, I'll scream. It's literally the only thing my customers want to talk about." The guy was all rich blond hair and intense green eyes, a mainstay waiter at Lumiere for looks and charm alone.

Mateo shrugged. "I'm just saying, best get to the grocery stores before the hoarders suck the shelves dry."

"Instead of the high school gossip session, you could be getting me that reduction, Sky," Bill called from the main station.

Sky let out a low breath. "Working on it, boss," she called, stirring the simmering reduction before her that started to take on the right velvety texture. She cast a sideways glance to Mateo. "If it makes you feel better, doll, I'll run to the grocery store tomorrow morning."

Tonight post-work, she'd agreed to hit Renegade Bar in downtown Wilmington with her best friend Aubs for a singles prowl. She'd spent enough time in one of the few Wilmington gay bars to get comfortable, but she hated putting herself out there in any capacity that wasn't friendly. To make matters worse, Mia asked to join them tonight, and Sky didn't have the strength to say no.

Just needed to get through this evening rush first.

***

Sky was grateful she'd packed a change of clothes, even though she reeked of sweat and spices from her shift. At least she'd been able to tone down the stench a little bit. She slowed as she strode closer to the entrance of Renegade's bar, a classy black exterior with rainbow flag decals on both of the windows. Music pumped from inside the building, loud enough to vibrate the glass.

She skimmed her fingers through her short strands, trying to smooth out the strays before she entered. Not like her tank top and flannel ensemble with beat-up cargos would win over any stunners tonight.

Not like she even wanted to with Mia in the room.

Sky stepped inside, the scents of the bar washing over her, all whiskey, pine, and clove from the arrangements Selina kept hanging throughout the place, like some kitchen witch. The crowds grew thick at this time of night, more than a couple of crews arranging themselves by the barstools. Normally, she and Aubs camped out there, and once in a while, Kyle. But the third member of their trio lived in Philly, so they caught her more often when they hit the bars there. Today, she found Aubs sitting in one of the high-backed booths lining the side of the bar. All the way in the back, the music pumped out even louder as a few guys and girls writhed around on the polished dance floor.

"Aubs," Sky shouted as she made her way over. She scanned the whole place, but she hadn't caught sight of Mia. Her gaze snagged on the booths lining the illuminated brick walls, but Mia wasn't sitting in any of those. Aubs finally made eye contact with her and gave a jerk of her head to signal "no."

Oh, fuck that. She wouldn't vag-block Aubs, but she hadn't arrived to hang out by her lonesome.

She stepped in front of their booth to spot the very woman she'd been searching for.

Mia sat across from Aubrey, looking as gorgeous as ever. She'd dressed up in a floral pattern tunic with black leggings that highlighted her slender form. Her hair tumbled to her shoulders in smooth mahogany waves, and the deep rose color of her lips mesmerized.

"Sky," Mia exclaimed, turning to face her. She patted the seat beside her. "Come and sit with us."

She couldn't help the bit of smugness that rose in her chest as she slipped into the booth beside Mia. Now she had no problem vag-blocking Aubrey.

Aubrey's jaw dropped, and she glanced between the two of them. "This is the friend you were waiting for?" She shook her head with a rueful grin, recovering from her surprise fast.

Mia leaned in against her, resting her head on Sky's shoulder. God, she forgot how touchy-feely her best friend could be and how much the skin-to-skin connection made her yearn. Warmth bloomed as simple as the flick of a lighter. Sky couldn't help indulging in this moment, weaving her arm around Mia's shoulders.

"Yeah, Sky invited me along. She said she was meeting a friend here," Mia responded.

Sky's lips twitched as she stared at Aubrey. "Mia, this is Aubrey, the friend I was meeting here."

Mia shot up in her seat, pulling away from Sky. Even as she dropped her arm, she couldn't help the pang of insecurity rolling through her. A model-caliber girl like Mia would last two seconds in a bar like this—Aubs alone was proof.

Aubrey Moore had long dark hair she kept back in a sporty ponytail, slender, pointed features, and a stunning body—half marathon running and half MMA. With looks like those, she'd made turning straight women into her favorite pastime.

Mia arched an eyebrow. "I thought you said you were here by your lonesome."

Aubs shrugged, a glint in her hazel eyes. "I'd say almost anything to get to talk to a babe like you a little longer."

Mia's cheeks flushed, and bile rose in Sky's throat, melding with irritation. She should've explained to Aubrey who this was before the woman started turning her full charms on to Mia. While her other best friend flirted as fast as she tipped back whiskey and tended to go through women like tampons, she was loyal to those she cared about. She'd met Kyle and Aubrey a few years ago, and the three of them had been inseparable since.

"Well, damn, now you've got me all flustered," Mia responded. Even as she said that, her thigh pressed against Sky's, a solid warmth she didn't dare budge from. "How long have you known my Sky? Clearly not during her high school years or we would've met."

Now it was Sky's turn to flush at the possessive term coming from Mia's lips. She'd ached to be hers for as long as she could remember.

Aubs eyes widened, and then she directed her questioning gaze to Sky.

Sky chewed on her lip and offered a nod.

Aubs took in a deep breath, and Sky relaxed. She now understood. Sky had rambled on about Mia at length to Aubs in the past, the mixture of high school fantasy and girl who got away she'd never quite moved on from.

Aubs leaned against the booth and took a sip from her gin and tonic. "I've known Sky ever since I tried to pick her up in this bar and she didn't get that I was aiming for a hookup until we'd reached her apartment and I tried to kiss her."

Sky snorted. "You're far too smooth, babe. Went right over my head."

Mia's thigh hadn't budged. If anything, she'd inched closer. Even as Sky pretended to focus front and center, she could only feel the point of connection where they touched, like she'd thrust her hand in an open flame and watched it burn.

"Yeah, the second we kissed, we both realized it felt weird and ended up spending the night watching *The*

Gingerdead Man and *Troll 2*," Aubs teased. "Sky and I were always destined to be besties."

The tension from Mia was imperceptible, but with their legs pressed, she could feel it. Plus, the lack of a bright smile on the woman's face offered the other indicator. Was she jealous? A moment later, Mia relaxed and pasted a grin on, but the smile dimmed compared to the blinders she normally delivered.

"I'm glad Sky's met someone as awesome as you. I've been on the other side of the country in Seattle, so you can imagine how much I've missed her." At that, Mia slung her arm around Sky's shoulders with enough force to feel a smidge possessive. Aubs cast Sky another quick glance, her brows raised. So, she wasn't the only one who'd noticed. If she knew Aubrey Moore, the woman would be blowing up her phone tomorrow with questions.

"Hey, I'm glad the two of you got the chance to meet," Sky said, trying to break through some of this awkward tension that descended. Mia had never gotten jealous of her other friends before, but then again, there hadn't been much opportunity. They'd been inseparable during high school, and her dating options consisted of a whole lot of nobody.

"Sky's told me you're recently single?" Aubrey

asked, fixing her attention on Mia. "Next time we can hit up a regular bar to play wingman for you too."

Mia shrugged. "Here works just as well for me too. My ex might've been a guy, but I play both sides of the field."

Now was Sky's turn to tense. A flush ran through her entire body, amping her up to Death Valley temps. Her mouth went dry with want. Back in high school, she'd always wondered but never worked up the nerve to ask if Mia was straight or not. The woman had one boyfriend senior year, which hadn't lasted long, and she rarely went on dates. Meanwhile, Sky had been out and proud, so she always figured if Mia was bi, she'd tell her.

Apparently not.

Aubs lifted her brows again, a slight grin playing on her lips. "Damn girl, a place like this you'll be like catnip, bringing all the pussy out to play."

Mia ducked her head, scratching the back of her neck. "I don't know if I'd be any good at the one-night stand thing. I'm way more the committed-relationship type."

"So, similar to our girl Sky here," Aubs said, jerking a thumb in her direction. Sky grew torn between gratitude and the urge to smack her friend's drink over. "Both of Sky's exes were year-and-change relationships, and I can't convince her to go prowl the bars with me for some 'one and dones.'"

Mia cast her an intense look, the smile on her face genuine this time. "Sky's always been like that. It's one of the many fan-fucking-tastic things about her."

"Is it getting hot in here?" Sky mumbled, unable to handle the sheer amount of heat pumping through her body right now. Though she hated to sever the contact with Mia, she didn't want to pour buckets of sweat on the woman either. She tugged off her hoodie and stuffed it on her opposite side. Mia's arm swept down, but her hand ended up resting on top of Sky's.

All of this touching pushed her to the point of deliriousness. She didn't need a single drink to amplify the lightheadedness swirling through her with Mia at her side, touching her like she couldn't get enough. Mia had always been physically affectionate, though, and chances were, Sky's distant daydreams were just getting the better of her.

Still, Mia was into women now. Questions flooded through her mind, too many to tackle at once. One kept surfacing over and over again: When?

Aubs cast her another smirky look before scanning the line of women over by the bar. Her gaze stopped on a lithe sweetheart with dark black hair and crimson lips who sat by her herself nursing a cosmo. The combo was Aubrey's kryptonite.

Aubs slapped a hand to the tabletop. "Well, ladies. Sorry to dine and dash, but destiny calls." She pushed up from the table, but before Aubs left, she passed another all too clear glance between her and Mia.

"Is she heading over to sweet-talk the woman there?" Mia asked, not moving her hand that pressed on top of Sky's.

"That's Aubs for you." Sky shrugged, casting a glance at Mia's empty glass. "Did you want another drink?"

"You haven't even gotten one yet," Mia said. "Let me grab you something."

"Babe, you go up there yourself and you're going to get swarmed," Sky responded. Already, the idea of watching half of the hungry women on the prowl approach Mia got her blood simmering. Great news, because Mia wasn't hers to get jealous over.

Mia squeezed Sky's hand. "Then you'll just have to protect me."

The sultry pitch of her voice sent Sky reeling. Before she could process the words, she stood from her seat, as if she had a shot in hell of collecting herself. Mia slid out after her, those azure eyes the sort of intense to throw her off-kilter.

If Sky had been more like Aubs, maybe she could read signals from other women. Maybe she could've interpreted Mia's actions ever since they'd collided back into each other's lives. However, if she was wrong—if this was Mia being extra friendly—she'd never recover from the embarrassment.

Not like she had the stones to confess when she truly liked someone. Both of her girlfriends had made the first move in her past relationships, and they'd both gotten tired over the same thing. Time and time again, Sky held back when she should be offering more of herself.

As they headed toward the bar, Sky slipped her arm around Mia's shoulders, pretending for a moment that this might be normal between them. As if all those fantasies weren't just wishful dreams and Mia might feel something more than friendship for her. Though truth be told, if those fantasies ever came true, she'd probably run screaming. She'd avoided anything true since her junior year.

One loss had been enough to ruin her for good.

She caught a couple of folks glancing at them upon approach. Once they caught Sky's arm wrapped around Mia and the way she leaned in as if they always did this, they returned to their conversations.

Sky squeezed them up to the bar, and Heather moseyed on over, offering a dusky grin.

"Jenkins, you have company tonight?" Heather called over the steady stream of chatter. "What can I get the two of you?"

"Jack and ginger for me," Sky ordered before leaning in against Mia. "What did you want?"

"What do you think?" Mia asked, her eyes glinting with amusement. As she spoke, her breath puffed against Sky's cheeks, sending a sinful shudder down her spine.

Sky took a moment, pursed her lips, and scanned her over, as if she didn't know what her best friend liked. Granted, in all the time they'd spent apart, her tastes might have changed. Sky took the risk anyway. "Do you trust me?"

Mia's lips curled in a delicious way that made her heart ache. She nodded.

"Amaretto sour," she called to Heather, who nodded and set to work at once. Before she could wrestle up some cash, Mia beat her to it, slipping the bill across the countertop. Heather snagged the cash with a wink.

"Why the Amaretto sour?" Mia asked, leaning in close enough for her lips to whisper across Sky's ear.

"Because of the night we stole your mom's bottle of

Amaretto and drank it at the park," Sky murmured. "You declared this was the only thing you ever wanted to drink again."

Mia's eyes lit, and her grin widened. "Perfect choice." Her whole body pressed against Sky's in a way that scorched every other thought from her mind. In this moment, the bar chatter faded away, the movement around them dissipated, and they stood in perfect stillness. In this moment, she could feel the warmth radiating off Mia's body and the velvet of her bare arms, the scent of her peach perfume lingering in the air.

In this moment, she could pretend Mia Brownstone was hers.

CHAPTER FOUR

MIA STRAIGHTENED FROM HER CROUCH IN FRONT OF the computer. Sky's rarely used desk and chair in her side room weren't bad, but they couldn't substitute for the ergonomic ones she'd owned back in Seattle. Once she settled into her own place, that was the first purchase she would make.

Her phone buzzed with an email from the property she'd found to rent. The two-story with the stone exterior on the outskirts of Wilmington went up for rental, and the moment she stepped inside, she'd fallen in love. With the broad, sprawling lawn, the open, airy kitchen, and the rounded doorways, the place oozed with charm, big enough to spur daydreams of settling down in.

Given the current spread of the TELA virus and the

government's new orders, we're going to postpone the move-in date for two weeks until we can get the place properly decontaminated. We're concerned the last tenant had contracted the flu before they left.

Thanks, Rachel

Mia's chest sank. Anxiety buzzed in the back of her mind at every mention of the virus, though she was one of the few in a lucky position where she already worked from home. Even if they started enacting some restrictions, she'd be okay. Except Sky had been too sweet to let her crash this long, and she hated imposing any more. If she were honest, the time with Sky healed her in ways she couldn't have imagined. She hadn't thought about Derek's stupid face most of this week, and the chorus of self-loathing that paraded through her head diminished. For the first time in a long, long while, she felt like someone cared.

She shut off her work laptop, closing out her shift for the day, and she stepped out of the side room. Mia made her way to the futon. Tonight, she'd be eating dinner by herself since Sky worked a full shift over at Lumiere, so she'd ordered a pizza. Then Mia would have to break the awkward news. When had this virus gotten so bad? The downside of not having an office to report in to meant she was behind on the news, but based on the ransacked state of the grocery store she swung out to yesterday, folks had descended into a full-fledged panic.

The rattle of keys sounded at the door, and a moment later, it creaked open. Mia sat up on the futon. As far as she knew, the only people who had keys to this apartment were her and Sky.

Sky burst inside, her footsteps slamming against the ground, and her shoulders heaving as if she were out of breath.

"Fuck, fuck, fuck, fuck," exploded from her, the door swinging shut from behind. Sky dropped to her knees and curled over. The sheer pain radiating off her slapped onto Mia like a paint splatter.

Mia barely felt herself move, but she rose from her seat and strode over to where Sky crouched, hands balled into fists on the carpet. Mia's stomach fluttered with nerves as she sank onto her knees beside Sky. Comforting her friend came naturally, even though they'd spent so long apart. Somehow their connection clicked into place like no time had passed.

Sky hadn't said anything since the outburst, her breaths heaving from her like shrapnel, while her fists curled so tight her knuckles looked like snowcaps. Mia rested a palm on her back, moving with careful measure so as not to surprise her. Sky's body tensed for a moment at the contact, but then she relaxed. Mia didn't say anything for a little bit, just stroking Sky's back until her breaths evened. Her throat squeezed tight at the panic bursting from Sky's pores.

Sky sucked in a shaky breath and began to sit up, but Mia moved her hand to Sky's shoulder, continuing to rub in small circles.

"Sorry," Sky muttered, ducking her head. She ran fingers through her thick brown hair, the sharp and short ends accenting her gorgeous face even more. Sky glanced at her, those dark brown eyes big and apologetic. "I'd been holding that in the entire walk home, and the second I stepped inside, it came pouring out. I didn't mean to scare you."

Mia offered a soft grin, not pulling away in the slightest. "You're going to have to try a lot harder to scare me, beautiful."

Sky hunched forward, balancing her elbows on her knees. "The governor issued a mandate to nonessential businesses, so everyone's inside to avoid further contact to spread the TELA virus. And I get it, the spread's real bad. But Lumiere's shutting down for the next two weeks—potentially longer, which means I'm jobless with no fucking income."

Mia nodded, Sky's words clicking into place as she processed. "What if I needed to a place to stay for two more weeks? I could pay rent?"

Sky's brows tugged together as she stared at her.

"My landlord told me I can't move in yet, which means I've got remote work that's unaffected by all of this and rent income that isn't going to them. If you'd be willing to put up with me for a bit longer, I'd be happy to pay." The worry deflated from Mia's chest at the simple solution. She'd take any chance to help Sky the way the woman helped her, even in a small way.

Sky pulled up from her hunch, severing the contact between them. Her breaths had calmed at this point, and she scrutinized her as if Mia was selling a junker used car. "Babe, I don't want you to feel like you need to bail me out."

Mia shook her head. None of that nonsense. "I'm offering payment for services rendered. We only agreed on me crashing a few weeks, and I'm mucking up your routine and taking your space for close to a month."

Sky let out another sharp breath. "I don't want to start this precedent between us...." She trailed off.

Mia nudged her foot against Sky's. "You're not. You never charged me rent, and I'm offering because this circumstance is shit. Think of it as me being greedy and wanting to keep a roof over my head while we're quarantined together."

Relief flooded her chest at the thought of being

quarantined with Sky. If she had already moved into her new place and been by her lonesome, she might've wilted away. Besides, she couldn't seem to keep her hands off Sky while they lived together. She'd always needed touch, but she'd never been this bad before. Part of the constant reaching out might have to do with the rising insecurities after Derek dumped her and everyone abandoned her. However, part of it might also be that she felt a thrum of attraction with every glimpse in the woman's direction.

Whenever Sky entered the room, Mia found her breath catching, her heart speeding up, and her whole body growing aware.

A buzz came from the door.

"And that would be the pizza," Mia said, tilting her head. "Want any?" she asked as she headed over to answer the door. Some rustling sounded behind her as Sky probably pulled herself off the floor. She cracked the door open and snagged the box the delivery guy thrust in her face. Her stomach rumbled at the scent of sausage and cheese. "Thanks," she called after him even as he bolted away. One thing she missed from her hometown was Vito's sausage and pepper pizza, and tonight she'd get to crack into the greasy delight once again.

Mia swung around and brought the pizza over to the counter.

Sky had begun unbuttoning the chef's jacket she wore, sliding it off her shoulders. Mia stopped in her tracks, a flush rising to her cheeks. The woman gained some serious muscle in their time apart, and the full tattoo sleeves up and down her arms made Mia want to spend hours exploring all the individual details. The thin white tank top Sky wore clung to her muscular body, placing her abs and curves on clear display.

Sky looked up, and their eyes met.

That flush spread through Mia's whole body as she glanced away, cracking open the pizza box as if food might offer some distraction. The scents barraged her at once, and Sky fished around in her pockets to pull out some cash. She slapped it on the countertop.

"If you're going to be covering rent, then I'm going to take over cooking duties while we're quarantined," Sky said, stepping in close.

"Oh, thank God," Mia responded with a grin. "I'm pretty sure I exhausted my recipe list at tacos, grilled cheese, and party dips."

Sky shook her head, an amused smile clinging to those full lips. "And of course you ordered sausage and pepper pizza. You haven't changed a bit, Mia Brownstone."

"Hope that's a good thing," she responded, grabbing two plates and setting them out on the countertop with a clink. "If I've got the same annoying traits I did as a teen, no wonder everyone was anxious to get rid of me back in Seattle." Even as the self-deprecating words escaped her lips, they left the stain of those fears that had risen inside her ever since she left.

She didn't look up, but she could feel Sky's demeanor shift. "What are you talking about, babe?" Sky's voice grew husky and low with concern.

A shiver ran down Mia's spine as she loaded pieces of pizza on plates and handed one over to Sky, looking up at last. The concern in Sky's eyes stabbed through her like tines of a fork. Not like she'd ever been good at hiding her feelings.

Mia tilted her head toward the couch they'd been eating on. "This is more of a sit-down conversation type of thing. Plus, don't want the pizza getting cold."

Her skin prickled at the idea of talking about anything from back in Seattle. For some reason, her time there grew distant the moment she moved home, and all her memories of Delaware came flooding back, like Seattle had been some temporary dream that morphed into a nightmare. Mia settled on the couch and took the first bite of her pizza.

The flavors exploded on her tongue, the salt and

sage of the sausage, the sweetness of the peppers, and the savory punch of the sauce. This familiar taste bolstered her confidence, giving her the strength to speak up. A moan slipped from her lips, and she forced herself to separate from the slice of pizza before she devoured the rest.

When she glanced up, Sky's eyes zeroed in on her with an intensity that made her shift in her seat. She hadn't touched her slice yet. Sky pursed her lips. "Making sexy noises at your pizza isn't going to deter me, Mia B."

Mia licked her lips. Clearly the sound had distracted her though. Ever since she returned, she'd been questioning the long, lingering glances between them. God, if only.

"I made most of my friends back in college, and Derek and I were part of the same group, you know? It was just the shitty thing about breakups. No matter how many people say they aren't going to choose sides, they always end up showing their true colors." Mia shrugged, trying to push away the tidal wave of sadness threatening to crest. She'd believed all of those friends to be true and reliable, but she'd been throwing herself headfirst into friendships from the time she'd grown old enough to scab her knees. She ended up scraping her knees a lot along the way.

Sky nudged her thigh against Mia's, as if she knew how much she needed the connection right now. "You do know if I had to choose anyone, it'd always be you." Sky's scent, all cedar and spice, had her full attention, causing her chest to stir.

Heat pricked Mia's eyes, and she swallowed hard. Her heart nearly leapt out of her chest at the one comment she'd needed to hear. She took another bite of pizza to try and keep the tears penned back. "Well, that's because you're the best person I've ever met, Skylar Jenkins. I was an idiot to go across the country for college, and I was an even bigger idiot to lose contact with you."

Sky nudged her leg again, but this time, their thighs remained pressed together. "Enough beating yourself up. You've always given all of yourself in your relationships, so don't pretend the way they ditched you didn't hurt. I don't fault you for finding local friends where you were—I did the same."

"Yeah, except once Derek didn't want me as his girlfriend anymore, the rest of them found excuses not to hang that got flimsier and flimsier. Guess the appeal wore out when I wasn't attached to him. Tough blow to the ego though," Mia murmured. "So yeah, there wasn't a single reason I could find to stay in Seattle." Her chest churned with all of those memories, the "can't tonights" when she'd later see pictures of them out at their local bars with Derek.

Sky took a bite of her pizza, chewing thoughtfully. "I never had to worry about that," she responded between bites. "With the whopping five friends I have, they wouldn't go abandon me for the rare girlfriend I brought around."

Mia shook her head. "I'm shocked you're not swarmed. Successful chef with the best sense of humor on the planet and straight-up gorgeous? I would've guessed you'd be turning down women left and right."

"There's nothing straight about me, babe," Sky responded, the huskiness in her voice sending a shiver down Mia's spine. "But no," she continued. "You forgot a workaholic who only talks about her cats and crumbles when someone tries to hit on her. Not the best selling points."

"Sounds like a dream to me," Mia responded before she could catch herself. She couldn't help but flirt with Sky, even though she shouldn't. This was her best friend, someone who she'd just reconnected with, yet everything came out of her mouth suggestively. It didn't help that ever since she'd cracked the code that she was bisexual, she'd realized what the very strong attraction to her best friend back in high school meant.

Sky's cheeks pinked as she wolfed down more of the pizza. For a few moments, they ate in silence, dodging the occasional paw from Shelley and Byron.

"Well, I'm glad you think so at least," Sky responded at last. "Because you're about to spend two more weeks confined with all of this," she said, gesturing from head to toe.

A furnace roared in Mia's chest, followed by a dizzying spin at the sheer proximity of the sexy woman, at the way their thighs touched.

Two weeks of close confinement with Skylar Jenkins.

If she survived this without crossing the line into brand-new territory between them and ruining her friendship for good, it'd be a miracle.

CHAPTER FIVE

DAY ONE OF THE OFFICIAL QUARANTINE PASSED WHILE Mia worked and Sky silently lost her mind.

Sky had scanned website after website for temporary jobs she might be able to swing, but her skill set classified more toward tangible, in-person jobs than anything that could translate to remote. They had enough food in the house to prep some decent dinners, so after half a day of job hunting online, she spent the second part of her day cleaning out her pantry and preparing a chicken jambalaya.

Mia worked in the side room today to take her IT calls, and every once in awhile, Sky could hear her through the door, explaining complex technobabble to an employee in a patient, icing-sweet tone. Yesterday, Sky was confident her world would be cracking to pieces, yet Mia offered not just a solution but the comfort she'd so sorely needed.

The woman was dangerous.

As much as Mia reassured Sky she'd returned to the area for good, part of Sky couldn't forget how fast Mia lost her number when she'd moved away. Mia had talked about a couple of out-of-state options for college, but Sky never believed her until one day she packed up and left. Sky had never done well with anyone leaving, not after she lost Jamie.

Her life felt like a revolving door, to the point she let few in now, yet she couldn't help welcoming Mia back with open arms, even if she might hurt her all over again.

The holy trinity simmered, and Sky gathered her ingredients together to make one of her favorite dishes. The homemade creole spice mix she kept on hand was one she loved. She'd kill to go to New Orleans and try the cuisine firsthand, but in the meanwhile, she'd continue to make the recipes Henri taught her at the first restaurant she worked at. She poured in the stock next, followed by the rice and the pieces of chicken before placing a lid over the top. Sky leaned against the counter, feeling at home in the kitchen, even if she rarely used hers.

The door to the side room creaked open, and Sky glanced to the clock over her stovetop.

"Finally done for the day," Mia said, stretching her arms overhead. The woman was determined to kill her, wearing a lace camisole that left plenty of skin exposed and skintight yoga pants that revealed the sloping curves of her hips and long legs. With her wavy chestnut hair pulled into a low bun, she looked as stunning as ever, and goddamn, Sky was staring slack-jawed again.

Mia traipsed over and leaned in against her. Sky swung her arm around Mia's shoulders as she'd started to do more and more as of late. Her apartment wasn't some vaulted ceiling penthouse by any means, and even if the place had been, extra space wouldn't have mattered. They both seemed to find any excuse to reach out and touch. As much as Sky hated to admit, she missed the casual caresses and the comfort they brought more than she realized.

"What are you cooking?" Mia asked. She took in a deep inhale. "Whatever it is, that smells amazing."

"Hope you like Cajun cooking," Sky responded. "Because we're having jambalaya tonight."

"Damn, you're fancy. How the hell did you let me cook the other days?" Mia asked, poking her in the side.

Sky snorted. "Because when you cook for work, the last thing you want to do is cook at home. However, now that I'm out of a job until this is over, I need my fix of being in the kitchen."

"You're a damn catch, Miss Jenkins," Mia said, pivoting toward her. "I'm going to grab a shower before we eat. Try to wash the irritating phone calls off my skin."

Sky managed a nod, even though she didn't need the mental image of her best friend naked to feed the flames coursing through her. She whipped toward the simmering pot on the stovetop and pulled off the cover, even though the jambalaya hadn't finished quite yet. The steam bathed her face, as if it stood a chance at masking the semi-permanent blush that graced her cheeks.

Two weeks of close confinement. God, she was screwed.

***

"I LET YOU PICK THE MOVIE TONIGHT, AND YOU CHOOSE *Legend?*" Mia slapped Sky in the side with a throw pillow.

Sky leaned into the couch, spreading her arms out over the top in an attempt to not curl in against Mia, who sat dangerously close. The heady proximity had gotten to her, and her nipples hardened to the point they threatened to launch missiles.

"I regret nothing," she responded with a grin.

"I guess it's worth watching for Tim Curry alone," Mia said, sinking back along with her. Inches separated them, and Sky had snuck at least a dozen glances in Mia's direction, soaking in the way the lace camisole glued to her stunning cream skin, highlighting the dip and curve of her breasts.

"Don't forget about Mia Sera in the gorgeous black dress," Sky responded. "That was a sexual awakening for me."

Mia fanned herself. "You and me both, beautiful."

Sky's tongue traveled over her lips as she shook her head. "How come I never knew this about you? We talked about everything back then, and you know I was one of the few out lesbians in our school. I thought out of everyone you might've come to me." Her heart twisted a little sharper. If Mia had known she was bi all of those years, maybe she'd never been interested in the first place and all of Sky's fantasies were just that.

Mia pulled her knees to her chest, hugging them tight. "I was kind of on autopilot in high school, I guess. You know my dad had left right before my freshman year, and my mom was more anti-relationship than ever. I just never considered it or explored my sexuality much, if that makes sense. Hell, I didn't even lose my virginity until the summer of my senior year."

Sky remembered the day Mia came rushing up to tell her about her first time with painful clarity. The last thing she'd wanted to hear about was Mia sleeping with anyone who wasn't her, but her best friend had been so excited. "So, you figured this out in college?"

Mia bobbed her head. "Before I started dating Derek, I had a three-month thing with this chick in my dorms. It kind of opened my eyes to a lot of shit I'd been blind to for most of my life."

Christ in hell, she shouldn't have asked. Jealousy sharpened her claws and sank them in. Her only solace was that she didn't know the woman Mia had gotten together with, but that didn't help much. Mia's ex-girlfriend was probably all sorts of confident with model looks—everything Sky wasn't. Sky's lips remained frozen. She should say something, but she couldn't admit anything that didn't sound hopelessly bitter. Sky turned her attention to the movie, an astronomical amount of glitter dominating the screen.

She could see Mia staring at her in her peripheral, those delicate brows drawn together. Sky tried to summon any words to her tongue that wouldn't seem like a total gear switch.

Mia's hand rested on her thigh, the heat from her palm soaking through the fabric of her jeans. "Hey, if I'd realized that about myself back in high school, you're the first person I would've told."

Sky chewed on her lip, offering a nod. Even in all their time apart, the woman still knew her better than anyone else. She glanced at Mia, who'd moved closer, so their thighs almost pressed against each other, knees touching. The woman hadn't removed her hand either, which made it impossible to process much with the way Sky's core throbbed at the touch.

Finally, she let out a sigh. "I didn't like thinking I might not have known you like I thought I did then."

Mia shook her head, her dark waves moving with the motion. She was all slender sensuality, a grace to her movements Sky could watch for hours—and had. "You knew me, all of me, Skylar Jenkins. I think you're about the only person in existence who can make the claim."

Sky chewed back the other words that leapt to her tongue. If she'd known Mia so well, how come she hadn't predicted the woman's cross-country move? The whole thing had shaken her so much at the time, she'd believed she would never recover.

"Besides, I'm not the only one who's made some changes in our time apart," Mia said, nudging her knee against Sky's. "When did you get all that ink?"

Sky glanced to her bare arms, which revealed the two full sleeves she'd gotten. She also had words wrapping around the side of her torso and plans with her tattoo artist to get a back design sketched out. She worked in an industry where tattoos were common—chefs never worked front of house, so no one cared if they inked up their bodies. And she'd fallen into the addiction full force.

Mia crawled closer, the view of her lace-covered breasts even better as she virtually climbed onto Sky's lap. She swallowed hard, hoping the woman couldn't hear the motorcycle rev of her heart.

"I guess over the past few years?" she said, trying to distract herself from the way Mia crouched right before her, knees dug into the cushion. "Once I started getting inked, I didn't want to stop."

"I don't have any myself," Mia said, her voice slow and deliberate. "But I've always found tattoos sexy."

The air may as well have evacuated the room. Mia's dark eyes filled with curiosity and an intent Sky couldn't quite discern, one that made her throat dry. Sky couldn't focus on anything but the woman before her, the movie playing in the background long forgotten. Mia's curves had gotten more pronounced with time, the freckles evident on her cheeks, and the Sagittarius pendant Sky had gotten her years ago still on a cord around her neck.

Sky reached out before she could help herself, her fingers pinching down on the hammered brass surface of the pendant. "Didn't think you'd still have this."

"I never take it off," Mia said as she shifted her weight on top of Sky's lap.

Oh hell. The reality of Mia sitting on her lap made her reel, warm legs pressing down on either side and that gorgeous body inches from her. She resisted the urge to wrap her arms around Mia's waist and dive in for her lips the way she'd been longing to for years now.

Mia's legs slipped to either side as the woman all but straddled her. "Who did your ink?" she asked, reaching forward to begin tracing the whorls of the pirate piece on her right arm, the rocking sea, the ship with bright sails, and the pirate girl in the forefront all done in detailed black and white linework. The feel of Mia's careful fingers skating across her skin made her delirious, to the point Sky almost forgot she'd ever asked a question.

"My friend from Needle and Ink up the street," Sky muttered, unable to keep the flush from her cheeks any longer. Not while Mia sat on her lap looking seductive enough that Sky's pussy ached. A delicious peaches and vanilla scent surrounded her. Sky exercised every ounce of her restraint to not close the distance between them.

Mia bit her lip, drawing Sky's attention to her face again, as if she needed more prompting to stare at this beautiful woman. Hell, those glossy pink lips looked like heaven. She'd sell her soul for a taste.

Mia shifted her legs, fingers switched to Sky's other arm as the movement forced Sky to bite back a moan. She'd have to spend some necessary time with her vibrator tonight after all of this.

"This one seems a lot more you." Mia's voice came out in a husky whisper, her fingers skating over the surface of Sky's arm as she traced over her linework. Not surprising she'd pay attention to this one—it had been her first piece. The stack of books trailed up her arm, opening into flying birds and a sunrise around her shoulder. She'd been a bookworm ever since she was a kid, and that one fixture in her life had never changed.

"Yeah," Sky murmured, wishing something cleverer would escape her lips. Instead, she made the mistake of looking up and catching Mia's eyes.

Mia's fingers froze in the middle of outlining the

tattoo on her left arm. The delicious weight of her on Sky's lap, the inches of tense air between them, and the electric feel of her fingers on her bare skin—everything had Sky soaked.

She'd opened this Pandora's box, and now she couldn't stuff her intense need away.

The air between them grew thick enough that each inhale was a struggle. Mia's chest heaved with each careful breath, as if one wrong move might shatter the tension between them. Her hips begged to be grabbed, close enough to require every remaining bit of self-control to resist.

Sky couldn't dare cross the line. Not when Mia had returned into her life. Not when it could ruin the friendship that just got rekindled.

Not when the inevitable rejection would break her.

Sky shifted in her seat, as if she could prompt Mia to get up without pushing her off. Instead, the movement brought Mia closer. She glanced up, trying to think of something to say, anything to get out of this compromising position with their friendship intact.

When her eyes locked with Mia's, the woman leaned in.

Her soft lips pressed to Sky's with a hesitant tentativeness that sent a thrill coursing through her veins. Sky's moan slipped from her lips, and her last thread of composure snapped. Her hands circled around Mia's waist, gripping slender hips tight as she kissed back with everything she'd been restraining. The woman tasted sweet, like honey and iced tea, and she indulged in the heat of her mouth. She explored her full lips and welcoming mouth with lazy strokes, drowning in the intensity.

Mia surrounded her, thighs pressed tight around hers, lips locked, and those fucking stunning breasts brushing against her own. The sensation made Sky's nipples tight, her underwear beyond soaked from the moment this gorgeous woman climbed onto her lap. Her fingers plunged into Mia's hair, gripping the silken strands as she devoured her mouth.

Mia might've been curious, but Sky was starving.

She kissed her with all of the longing that burned in her chest, an undying hearth for years now. Mia's delicious scent caused her mind to spill over the sides. Her fingers dug into Mia's hips, not wanting the woman to budge an inch from here.

Not wanting this to end—ever.

She'd imagined this moment a thousand times over, yet the reality tasted far sweeter, far more intoxicating… and far more dangerous.

The thought splashed cold water over the glorious

heat climbing up her skin in tendrils, spreading between them into a consuming inferno.

Sky pulled back, gasping for air, her shoulders heaving.

Mia's brows lifted, her eyes widening.

Sky chewed on her lip. Fuck, she couldn't wait around to see the regret on the woman's face. "I've got to go," she muttered, embarrassment coating her skin like oil.

Mia shifted off her lap, her brows drawing together and her mouth opening as if she might say something. Before she could, Sky pushed up from the couch and strode to her room like a fucking coward.

Just moments before, she'd soared higher than she could ever believe, and as she stepped inside her bedroom and closed the door behind her, she careened down.

Sky leaned against her door, wishing she hadn't pulled away. Wishing she was smoother, less vulnerable. Wishing she could be someone else.

One day into this quarantine and she'd fucked their relationship up for good.

CHAPTER SIX

Mia was never more grateful for her job than today.

Once she woke up this morning, she'd hidden away in the side room, bringing a bowl of Frosted Flakes in with her to minimize time in the kitchen. She'd mastered the necessary work voice even post-breakup and clung to that cheerful mask today. As if she stood a chance at fending off the demons rampant inside her head.

Honestly, she had no one to blame but herself. She slouched in the uncomfortable chair behind the small desk and heaved out a sigh. She'd just finished another long call with an employee who couldn't get into their email. That had been a temporary distraction, but when the click of the phone sounded, the memories of last night returned. She thought Sky had given her the same look back—that the tension in the air was mutual attraction.

Mia couldn't comprehend how passion like that could be faked. The moment their lips met, a switch flipped, and Sky had taken control. Mia could still feel the brand of her fingers digging into her hips and the way she devoured her mouth. Their kiss had been one of the most passionate of her life, and she'd entertained some memorable ones. Kissing Sky had been like watching the sunrise at the shore, tasting that salt breeze in the air, and witnessing those first tendrils of light that fluttered in her heart like hope.

Yet, something had spooked Sky.

The woman had been revving the motor down the highway at a hundred miles per hour, and then she'd made a fast break and turn, bolting for her bedroom. Mia hadn't even come down from the high of their kiss to process what Sky said before the door clicked shut.

Still, this was Skylar Jenkins she'd kissed, not some random hottie in her college dorm. This was one of the most important people in her life, and she'd gone and scuffed the line of friendship that always existed between them. This was the woman who'd opened her home to her when she needed help the most, even after Mia had been a shit friend for abandoning her in the first place.

Yet, the moment she'd knocked on the door and saw Sky again, all those deep, intense feelings she'd held for her best friend surfaced. Except this time, she understood what they were. This time, she was aware of how watching Sky maneuver in the kitchen made her flush. How every touch sent jolts of electricity through her veins. How the husky way Sky said "babe" slithered straight to her core.

Mia let out another sigh. She could've just kept her impulses in her pants and practiced some restraint. Not like they would be stuck together for the next two weeks with minimal places to escape or anything.

"Great job," she muttered to herself. From the other room, the creak of footsteps and the stomps from Sky's tabbies traveled to her. Part of her wanted to burst into the room and ask for a do-over of the last twenty-four hours—pretend the kiss never happened. The other part of her wanted to pop open the window and shout to the streets below that it had, because some people went entire lifetimes never experiencing a kiss like that.

She glanced at her empty mug of tea. Before she started on her next call, she should refill. Of course, heading out there meant facing Sky. However, she never ducked away from a challenge, even if mortification drained through her body at a steady drip. Last night had turned from life-altering to disastrous in mere moments.

Mia gritted her teeth and pushed up from the seat, grabbing the mug as if she donned armor. She was paying rent these next two weeks, and she had every right to use the kitchen, even if her heart slammed so hard she could hear it by the time she reached the door. She slipped out with barely a creak.

Sky stood in the middle of the kitchen unloading the dishwasher, unaware Mia had stepped out from the side room with the rattles and clanks coming from the plates and bowls. Byron slunk over to weave through her ankles, and she let the soft motion fill her with whatever confidence she could muster.

At this rate, she'd get used to feeling like an outsider everywhere she went, no matter how hard she tried.

Mia tiptoed over to the electric kettle, but when she pulled it up, she could feel Sky's gaze burning into her. This had been a bad plan.

"Just came out to get some tea," she said, lifting the kettle and making her way to the sink. Her skin prickled when Sky didn't say anything, even though she could feel the pressure of her stare. God, this was more mortifying than she'd imagined. She filled the kettle and then popped it on the stand, flipping the button on to steam up. Mia leaned with her back against the counter, folding her arms in front of her.

Sky stopped loading the dishwasher and leaned against the counter too. Their gazes locked, and Mia's breath snagged in her throat. Sky's deep chocolate eyes looked troubled, and she kept opening and closing her mouth as if trying to decide what to say.

Mia had done enough damage in kissing her best friend last night, so she would sit out on this one.

Sky's brows drew together. "Did you know that one bolt of lightning could toast a hundred thousand pieces of bread?" She scratched the nape of her neck, not looking at Mia.

For a moment, Mia stood there dumbfounded, but she'd known Sky long enough to understand what the comment was—an olive branch. She might not be ready to talk about last night yet, but she attempted to return to normalcy as best she could.

Even as her heart twisted, Mia couldn't help her wry grin. "And what would anyone want to do with that much toast?"

"Feed breakfast to a massive assembly?" Sky hazarded. She popped open the cabinet behind her. "What kind of tea did you want, Mia B?"

She'd been hoping for more, but if Sky was at least willing to play ball and keep things from getting awkward around here, she'd jump back in. Even though disappointment corroded her insides, she'd dealt with it before, and she would again.

"Pick one for me," Mia said, offering a hesitant smile, as if they could return to where their friendship was before she'd kissed Sky.

Sky's cheeks flushed, and she tugged out a bag of peach black tea, like she knew what Mia would be gunning for. Fuck, it would help if the woman wasn't so perfect. Sky walked over the bag of tea and popped it into her cup. With the close proximity, Sky's scent wafted by—the cedar and musk that inspired the physical sensations of last night.

Awkwardness settled between them, a blanket coating like the first snow of winter.

If they were going to get through this with their friendship intact, she needed to try too. "I'm shocked you have such a variety of tea, coffee queen."

Sky grinned. "I'm allowed to love both. I developed a taste for Earl Grey when I was in culinary school. Plus, cooking with tea is fascinating."

"Now *that* I want to try," Mia said, tipping the steaming kettle into the cup. "Not like the jambalaya you made last night wasn't next-level stuff. Is all New Orleans cooking that damn good?"

"You have no idea," Sky said, excitement flashing in her eyes. "New Orleans is a buffet of food diversity. I've always wanted to go down there and just eat my way through the city."

"Sounds amazing," Mia said, grabbing her mug. As much as she tried to get back to normal with Sky, her heart still ached. "Time to get back to the salt mines. Guaranteed I've got Deb on the phone again since she can never figure out the first thing about her work computer." She made her way to the door. Despite the lingering disappointment, relief flooded through her. They hadn't shattered apart after last night. Both of them were trying.

She paused at the door. "Old-school creative time tonight?" Mia asked.

Sky chewed on her lip and nodded. "And I'll cook dinner. Good luck with Deb."

At that, Mia disappeared into the bedroom.

Mia honestly hadn't drawn in years.

She'd wanted to major in art when she'd started college, but the first few classes were so restrictive and horrible that she jumped ship over to information technology. And Derek was more of the "going out to the bars and socializing" type than quiet creative, so she'd rarely stolen the moments to draw anything out like she used to.

Once she placed her pencil to the page tonight and sketched those first lines, a release flooded through her, familiar and thrilling at the same time. Music pumped through Sky's portable speakers as she played some soft acoustic while they both worked. Sky had an old notebook in front of her to toy around with some poetry, while Mia lugged out her dusty sketchbook.

Even though the frisson of tension still carried through the air between them, Sky did her damndest to make things normal, so Mia would too. Not like attraction had a shut-off valve though. She camped out on the futon while Sky sprawled out on the couch.

The woman leaned against the side of her couch, her knees up as she used them to prop her notebook. She'd dressed down in a thin gray tank top with no bra that kept drawing Mia's gaze, and her low-hanging black sweats exposed her gorgeous hipbones. Her smooth olive skin begged for a bite, and the way her lips pursed while she concentrated on the notebook in front of her sent Mia's heart fluttering.

Right, like she'd be able to stuff away this infatuation.

Mia sucked in a sharp breath and focused on the paper in front of her. She'd started simple with the idea to sketch a tree, but soon the lines had grown curves and features, turning into a dryad before her eyes. Each stroke of pencil to paper loosened something inside her, as if she tugged at a cord wrapped around her insides, slowly beginning to unravel it. She'd missed this outlet more than she'd realized.

After all of the time she spent finding herself in Seattle, she'd also lost parts of herself in the process. Currently, she wasn't sure who the hell she was anymore, and sometimes, when the toll of the push-aways and rejections grew too steep, she didn't feel like that person deserved anything, least of all love.

Sky's phone rang, and she rolled up from her couch to snag it. "It's the folks," she explained before heading into the other room.

Mia glanced at her own phone. Not a text from her mother yet, apart from her initial check-in when the governor issued the shelter-in-place mandate, which had given her the warm and fuzzies. She continued working on her sketch, drawing some of the lighter, slighter lines of intricate details, even though her gaze slipped over to the abandoned notebook on Sky's couch.

The temptation to sneak over there and take a peek into the inner workings of Sky's mind reared strong. However, in the past, Sky might have needed a few days, but she always ended up talking to Mia about the real stuff. Their situation had changed—hell, their friendship had—but one thing hadn't: she trusted Sky.

Still, the notebook sat on the couch mocking her with all of the untold secrets she needed to know.

A moment later, the door creaked open, and Sky strode over to the couch. "Mom and Dad say hi," she offered, collapsing back into the couch. "Mom's going a little stir crazy, but Dad's started a brand-new wood-working project."

Mia cracked a grin. She adored Sky's folks. They'd been the second family she'd never had—Sky, her parents, and Sky's sister Jamie. The loss of the youngest Jenkins had rocked through the whole family their junior year, and she wasn't sure any of them had ever recovered.

"Tell your mom if she needs to talk anyone's ear off, I volunteer as tribute," Mia offered, warmth spreading in her chest.

"She'll love that," Sky said, one of those heart-stealing grins gleaming in her eyes. "Plus, it means I'll be off the hook for constant phone chatter." Her gaze traveled toward Mia's phone, and her lips pursed, but she didn't ask the obvious. Mia's mother wouldn't call unless there was an emergency.

"What are you working on?" Mia asked, pushing up from the futon's embrace. God, she wanted to slip onto the couch beside Sky and just lean in, but she'd ruined the casual comfort between them.

"Some terrible poetry," Sky flashed a smile. "It's been a while since I flexed those muscles. You?"

"A dryad sketch, but I'm also ridiculously rusty." Mia paused, wanting to go further, to ask more, but that got her into trouble last night. They'd leapt into the deep end, and Sky swam away.

"I'm sure it's amazing," Sky murmured as she settled into place, propping up her notebook again. "Your sketches always spoke to me. You've got talent, Mia B."

Mia's cheeks heated. God, this woman. How could she move past her when she said things like this? Silence spread between them, half awkward tension and half the comfortable routine they'd slipped into earlier. Neither of them dared break the quiet this time. Sky retreated to her poetry while Mia returned to the dryad she sketched out, getting into the detail work she loved.

Hours passed, the chill acoustic music playing on in the background. Mia placed the finishing touches on her sketch, realizing she hadn't moved in far too long. Her limbs throbbed as she began to stretch them out in front of her. She hadn't gotten sucked into a task where everything melted away in ages. She'd missed this, almost as much as she'd missed Sky.

Mia cast a glance over to the couch.

Sky had dropped the notebook and curled onto her side. Her eyes were firmly shut, and her shoulders rose and fell with the steadiness of slumber. Mia slipped from her spot on the futon, pushing up to stretch her legs and then swing her arms overhead.

She grabbed one of the spare blankets piled on the floor and tiptoed her way over to where Sky lay on the couch. Mia snagged the notebook from the ground, shutting it before she caught the words inside—no matter how tempted she was. Sky lay there in perfect surrender, those deep pink lips parted with her breaths, her dark lashes standing out against her deep olive skin. She looked so beautiful lying here that Mia's heart ached.

She slid the blanket over Sky's shoulders, swallowing hard at the way the woman nestled in deeper afterward.

They'd been able to skate on shallow ice today and

pretend things remained normal, but the truth was, even if things hadn't shifted for Sky, they had for Mia.

Once she understood the depth of what she'd always felt for this woman, spending time around her caused those feelings to surface all the more. And even if she remained stuck with this hopeless longing, she couldn't pin it back any longer.

Skylar Jenkins made a mark on her heart long ago.

CHAPTER SEVEN

SKY HAD GOTTEN EVERYTHING SHE'D EVER HOPED FOR, and in one snap decision, she'd fucked that bright and beautiful chance with Mia up.

Typical.

Even though Mia played along with her superficial "everything's fine" game, she caught the lingering looks from the woman as well as the pause of hesitation every time they talked. Two days had passed, which meant the weekend arrived, and the buffer of Mia's job no longer worked.

Today, the tension ratcheted up a few notches—no matter how many weird facts about Ancient Rome she spouted or random offbeat Star Wars trivia she tried to combat the awkwardness with. She'd hurt Mia the other day, she'd hurt herself, and honestly, she didn't know how to climb out of that pit of despair.

Sky rubbed the towel through her still-drying hair before tossing on her pair of plaid pajama pants and a loose tank top. The thin fabric glued to her damp post-shower skin like paste. Out in the living room, she could hear shuffles and thumps from Mia. She didn't suppose drinking away the afternoon was an option. Maybe she'd find some answers at the bottom of a bottle.

Sky sucked in a sharp breath and tugged the door open. When she entered the main area, she stopped where she stood. Mia had cleared out space in the middle of the living room and worked through a circuit of intense cardio. She'd stripped to those shorts that left little to the imagination and a loose tee with the straps of a sports bra peeking out. Mia had broken into a sweat, and even though she offered a nod in acknowledgment, she didn't stop the drop-down push-ups or spring back ups in the middle of her workout.

Sky headed to the kitchen to grab Mia a glass of water for when she finished. The way she looked with her muscles flexing, sweat dripping down her body, and her clothes plastered to her body turned Sky on more than anything. If she hadn't been such a coward the other night, she wouldn't just be here watching in the aftermath. Hell, instead, maybe she'd be the one peeling the fabric off her and tasting the salt on her skin as she memorized Mia's body with her mouth.

The thought got Sky wet in seconds, and she clenched her thighs together to try and distract herself. Nope, instead, she sailed her away on her sinking failboat and pushed the woman she'd lusted after for years away. *Good move, champ.*

Sky focused on getting the glass of water and pouring herself another mug of coffee that she heated in the microwave. Even still, she noticed Mia in her peripheral, looking all sweaty and gorgeous, her hair pulled into a ponytail and stray strands glued to her forehead. The flush on her cheeks probably looked the same after she—

Oh, Jesus fuck. Head out of the gutter.

The soft sound of Mia's sharpened breaths wasn't helping Sky at all. She might as well just pour the ice water over her now—maybe the shock might pull her out.

Tonight. She'd nut up and have a real talk with Mia tonight.

Mia stilled, reaching the end of her workout. Her shoulders heaved, and sweat glistened across her creamy skin, a flush crawling up her from head to toe.

"Thirsty?" Sky asked, holding a cup of water. She withheld her grin. The thirsty one here was her.

Mia bobbed her head, trying to manage words between her heaving breaths. "Sorry for taking up the living room to get that out. I can't hit the gym right now, and I'm going out of my mind without the usual outlet. Besides, I'm living the single life right now, so I can't let myself go."

Sky lifted her brow. "Oh, shush. You're always gorgeous." Her cheeks pinked as she realized what she'd said out loud.

Mia's shoulders tightened, and she glanced away at first. "Yeah, well, I won't stay that way if I slack."

Sky swallowed hard. The flirting that had been so natural before now turned awkward in the wake of the kiss they'd shared and how Sky all but bolted from the room. She wanted to say something to smooth the rumpled tension over, but no words came out of her dry mouth. Instead, she thrust the glass of water in front of Mia.

"Here, drink," Sky instructed, as she grabbed her own cup of coffee and buried her face in it.

"All right, cavewoman," Mia responded, an amused grin lifting her lips. "Me drink water."

"I'm going simple tonight with a cassoulet," Sky said, skimming her fingers through her damp strands, as if she had a chance of dodging her discomfort right now.

Mia snorted. "Simple is burgers, beautiful. Not some fancy French dishes."

A sinful shudder ran down her spine whenever Mia called her beautiful, especially after she'd tasted those perfect lips. If she said she hadn't replayed their kiss every hour since it happened, she'd be a damn liar.

"Cassoulet's easy, not fancy," Sky protested. "I mean, the duck confit requires some prep-work, and I had the ragout and beans cooked up yesterday, but now I just need to assemble the components, which is simple."

Mia crossed her arms over her chest and crooked an eyebrow at her. "Look at all those fancy words you're spouting. You're talking to the takeout queen here."

Sky shook her head, a rueful grin on her lips. "If you ever want to learn, I'd be happy to show you the basics."

Mia's eyes widened, and her slow grin spread. "Yeah, I'd love that."

"And don't worry, I'm great at putting out kitchen fires," Sky teased.

Mia flipped her the finger. "One. Time."

Sky began pulling the containers from the fridge

and assembling them next to the stovetop where she'd be operating. While she adored cooking at Lumiere and loved the work she did, she found a fair amount of comfort in preparing dinners for her and Mia. If she'd been by her lonesome during this, she would've been dining on frozen burritos and pizza, uninspired to cook for herself.

Mia's phone rang. She pursed her lips and looked down at the screen. "Let me take this," she murmured, heading over to the futon to take a seat. Based on the storm clouds in her eyes, Sky could place a wild guess as to who was calling.

Sky focused on the prep-work in front of her, the delicious lemon and thyme scents of the duck confit wafting her way. The sausages began to fry on the pan with a sizzle, and she turned them over, getting them well cooked. In the other pot, she crisped the bread-crumbs, adding some duck fat in to give them an extra golden tone.

"Yes, I'm staying inside," Mia said on the futon, gripping her phone tight. Her voice grew terse. "I'm not homeless, Mom."

Sky's heart twisted. Mia and her mother's relation-ship had always been complicated. She'd met Ms. Brownstone a thousand times, and while the woman approved of her, Mia's mom contained the warmth of a freeze-pop. Her daughter was the polar opposite, brimming with downy softness and summer's heat, and all throughout high school, Sky watched Mia crave the affection she'd never gotten from her mother.

"If the virus gets worse, I'll still be here at Sky's," Mia responded, the tension permeating through the room. "No, I won't show up on your doorstep bringing the plague."

Sky busied herself with chopping the finished sausages and pulling the breadcrumbs off of the heat. The oven beeped as it finished preheating, and she layered the cassoulet in a massive dish. This meal would last them a few days, but then again, she loved the convenience of leftovers.

Mia's voice dropped lower to the point Sky could barely make out what she said. Mia had been dumped by her boyfriend, her mother pushed her away, and still she offered smiles and sunshine wherever she went. Sky's running away the other night probably added one more rejection onto the stack. She gripped the sides of the casserole container tight. She needed to make this right.

"Fine, Mom," Mia said. "You stay safe too." With that, she ended the call and sank into the futon.

Sky lowered the casserole into the oven and set the

timer before she made her way out of the kitchen and into the living room. Her heart hammered hard, but she approached anyway, dropping down into the futon beside Mia.

"Your mom called?" she asked, hesitation in her voice.

"Oh, did her blizzard travel all the way over to the kitchen?" Mia responded, her voice like the serrated edge of a knife. "Sorry for the frostbite. She tends to leave that."

Sky leaned in closer until their legs brushed together. "She'd give Mr. Freeze a run for his money."

Mia's eyes glossed over, and panic rose in Sky's chest.

Mia scrubbed at her eyes. "Don't worry, I'm not about to go bawling my eyes out. I'm just so tired of trying with folks and hoping someone—anyone might care about me as much as I do for them. Mom's only up to her usual shit."

Sky's heart broke then and there. She'd been guarding herself, and in the process hurt Mia, but sitting here witnessing how she tried to hold herself together—Sky crumbled.

Mia removed her hands from her eyes, which reddened from the tears she restrained. She cracked a wavering half-smile. "Sexy, right?"

Sky's heart thudded harder as she leaned in, tucking a stray strand of Mia's silken hair behind her ears. "You always are, babe," Sky murmured. They were inches apart, to the point she could feel Mia's breath puff against her skin, and she couldn't find the willpower to pull back.

"Not fucking fair," Mia huffed out, her smile faltering. "Look, I can accept you don't want me—par for the course with my life. But the flirting, Sky, it hurts." Sharp, fragmented pain radiated in Mia's Atlantic blues, pain Sky had put there.

God, she was such a fuck up. The last thing she wanted to do was make Mia feel the same hurt and fear.

Even though the words stuck in her mouth, she could do one thing right now. Sky leaned in closer until their lips were a whisper apart. The woman didn't move, but Sky could feel the intense stare on her, and she grew heady from the sheer focus. Mia's scent surrounded her, her warmth, like she brought the pale sunbeams indoors. Mia made the first move last time—which meant she needed to summon a little courage of her own.

Sky closed the distance between them, pressing her lips to Mia's.

The woman's mouth opened to hers at once, and

Mia kissed with a desperation that vibrated through her being. Sky wove her fingers through those satin strands, and she sank deeper into their kiss, the honeyed taste one she wanted to return to. Their lips met over and over again, the soft and sinful sensations coursing through her like the caress of hot water lapping around her skin or the balmy sweetness of a spring breeze.

Fear bubbled within her again, the same one that gripped her before. What if she ruined her friendship? What if Mia left her again?

Everyone always left.

Yet Sky pushed through, surrendering to the bliss of Mia's mouth against hers. She swept her tongue inside, elongating the kisses. She dragged each one out until they both surfaced for breath. Her heart hammered so loud she guaranteed her neighbors could hear, and an engine's heat roared inside her. She leaned in, desperate to drown herself in this kiss, and Mia began to slide onto her back, down to the futon.

Sky crawled over the top of her, bracing her hands around the gorgeous woman. Her thighs crowded around Mia's, and the ache in her pussy grew so needle-sharp and intense that her breath snagged. She'd gotten so turned on she was positively dripping.

Mia's curves pressed into her, and damn, she

wanted to touch the woman's velvet skin so badly. Sky memorized Mia's mouth with her lips in case this was just a fleeting dream, in case everything crumpled to fragments after this. Her nails curled into the fabric of the couch as their mouths came together again and again and again. She could taste the tang of their swollen lips, mingling with a sugar and cream sweetness she couldn't help but return to.

As she kissed Mia Brownstone, their bodies melded together in a way that felt perfect, and the years melted away. This was the culmination of every teenage fantasy brought to life, hours and hours spent daydreaming of this reality. Those memories grew so overwhelming they dizzied her mind—high-school Sky wasn't a version of herself she returned to often.

The sharp reminder of why she didn't return there pierced through, shattering the haze. Sky sucked in a cool breath. No. This time, she wouldn't run.

She pulled back from Mia, but she didn't move from where she hovered over her, palms pressing into the couch. She couldn't help but stare at the woman beneath her, those pink lips swollen from the way they'd made out, her ocean eyes a little lost and dreamy. The freckles dusting her cheeks were even clearer, and she still had the little scar on the far end of her right cheek from when she'd tripped into a thorn bush on one of their adventures.

Her heart swelled, and she couldn't bring herself to look away.

"I'm sorry for bolting the other night," Sky managed at last, the words feeling foreign on her tongue. "I got freaked out and panicked. You're my best friend, Mia, and I didn't want to jeopardize that."

Mia blinked, and a moment later, she reached up to trace her fingertips along Sky's cheeks with a gentleness that made her ache. "You'll never lose me, Skylar Jenkins."

Sky's throat thickened.

Mia might offer up the platitude, but the truth was, she had moved away, and if she hadn't gone through a breakup and returned home, Sky might've lost her.

Besides, she'd never forgotten the lesson she learned when Jamie left them—nothing lasted forever.

Those fears clogged her throat, but she couldn't pull herself away from Mia. This was everything she'd hoped for but also everything she feared most.

For the time being, she'd just have to hold onto this joy while she still had it.

CHAPTER EIGHT

MIA'S BODY STILL BUZZED AFTER THE KISS SHE'D SHARED with Sky last night. Their make-out session hadn't gone any further than that, but just the feel of Sky's body pressed against hers sent fantasies whirring into overdrive.

She pushed up from the futon at the sounds of the coffeemaker percolating. The rich scent of roasted beans traveled her way. As Mia headed over to the kitchen where Sky leaned against the countertop, she couldn't help the flush of awareness that rolled through her. Sky was the sort of fucking beautiful she couldn't get out of her mind. The shorter haircut and casual, boyish way she held herself always gave her a hot-as-hell vibe, but the depths in her dark eyes and the hesitance behind her words made her shine even more.

"Don't tell me you made me coffee," Mia said, announcing herself. "Be still, my heart."

Sky cracked a half-smile. "What do you mean for you, woman? This entire carafe is mine."

Electricity zipped through the air the moment their eyes met, and the heat in Sky's gaze was undeniable. How she'd mistaken it all these years mystified her. Mia snagged one of the bar stools on the breakfast nook as Sky pulled out mugs from the cupboards. Her heart thumped hard at sitting here in her proximity.

She'd kissed her best friend. And Sky had kissed her back. A grin bubbled inside her, a thrill she could barely contain. Not like she knew how to proceed now, though. Were they dating? Was this just a fling while they were quarantined together? She already wanted answers, but she still stung from how Sky had dashed from the first time they kissed.

She didn't want to scare her away again.

Was kissing a normal thing they could do now? Because hell on earth, she wanted to kiss Sky again. The woman pursed her lips as she poured the coffee into the mugs and then began doctoring them with half and half and sugar. Mia loved that she didn't even need to tell Sky what to put in hers. Sky understood her better than anyone else on this earth did.

Sky placed the mug of coffee in front of her, and Mia reached for it, her fingers brushing against Sky's in the process. The electricity that zinged at the simple touch was a revelation. Mia didn't want to pull away, but the mug had begun to scorch her palm. She brought the mug closer.

"What do you want to do today?" Sky asked. "Since we're both off rather than just me and my unemployed ass."

Mia glanced at the window. The early sun streamed through, beckoning her outdoors. Any normal day, they'd be able to run out, grab brunch, and stroll along the Riverwalk, one of her favorite places. However, with the quarantine restrictions, a lot of the parks had been shut down, and most businesses as well. The concept still seemed so foreign to her, something she could've never anticipated. She and Sky had made a pact to ignore the news as much as possible, which was one of the things keeping her afloat right now amid all the fear and panic permeating the country.

"Goddamn, we're living in the apocalypse," Mia murmured, taking the first sip of coffee. The rich, robust liquid warmed her throughout.

Sky sat on the stool beside her, the fragrance of cedar and spice making Mia's heart flutter. "You'd think we'd at least get zombies or riot gear. But no, lamest apocalypse ever. Everyone's stuck indoors."

"Are there any trails around here that might not be shut down?" Mia asked. "I'd kill to get outside today."

"Well, given it's just you and me here and I don't relish an untimely death, I think I can make something work," Sky teased, an amused glint in her eyes. "Let me slip on some actual pants and shoes."

Mia tipped back more coffee. The idea of getting outside of the apartment sent a jolt of exhilaration through her, but even more so, Sky's proximity got her pulse jumping. Sky's gaze lingered on her, so Mia made sure to trail her tongue over her lips nice and slow after she placed the mug down.

"And here I thought I knew you," Sky said, pushing from her seat on the stool. "I had no clue you were such a goddamned tease, Mia Brownstone."

"Only when I see something I like," she responded, her palms wrapped around the mug.

Sky's cheeks turned bright red, and she ducked her head. This woman was damn addictive. Mia couldn't help the small grin playing on her lips. She hadn't realized how thrilling flirting with this woman could be.

"Right, let me get changed," Sky said, striding toward her room and slipping inside.

Mia pushed off from her seat and headed over to her suitcase that lay beside the futon. She'd already done laundry, but she got sick of wearing the same five outfits over and over again. In a few deft motions, she stripped out of the shorts she'd been wearing to sleep in and popped the tank top overhead, tossing both into the suitcase.

Mia slipped on a fresh pair of underwear and strapped her unimpressive tits into a bra. She tackled a pair of leggings next. Honestly, the fresh clothing felt better than she expected. The door to Sky's room creaked open right as she lifted her olive-green tunic to slip it on. Sky's eyes locked with hers, and they both froze. She didn't miss the way Sky's heated gaze raked over her body, and she was tempted to just say fuck it, throw the shirt to the floor, and sprawl out on the futon in invitation.

Mia sucked in a deep breath and tugged the tunic up and over. God, she'd never been this obsessed before. Sex with her partners in the past had its ups and downs, but the strength of her attraction to Sky was brand new. The depth reminded her of standing at the Riverwalk in the middle of summer, the balmy breezes whipping around her and making her feel glorious, free, and infinitesimal in the wake of the beauty surrounding her.

"Sorry," Sky muttered, heading over to the kitchen counter to bury her face in her mug of coffee.

Mia's lips curled into a smile. Her core throbbed at all of the filthy fantasies rolling through her mind right now. "Nothing to be sorry about," she responded as she finished slipping socks and shoes on. When their gazes locked again, Mia didn't look away, a newfound brazenness rising inside her. "Let's get outside. I don't want to miss another second of sunshine."

"I don't think it's going anywhere fast," Sky responded, her crooked grin causing Mia's heart to squeeze tight. Sky tilted her head toward the door and snagged her keys with a jangle. "All ready when you are."

Within a few minutes, they'd exited the apartment building, and Mia took her first big breath of the outside air. The sunlight shone down on her, warming the earth for early spring. She could feel the beams sink in past her skin, flooding through her with a golden lightness that she adored. The breeze smelled like honeysuckle and moss, even in the middle of the city. Few cars roamed the streets, and the sidewalks were empty apart from a few folks walking their pups.

Sky led the way, swinging her arms as she walked. Mia hurried to catch up with her long strides. They traveled down one of the side streets and then another until they headed in a familiar direction. She might've grown up in Talleyville, out in the 'burbs of Wilmington, but she'd whiled away enough hours in town through high school to know every inch of this city.

"Spend a little time out here and I can almost forget I'm out of work and in isolation," Sky said, her arms still swinging as she walked. She stared at the sky, wonder gleaming in her dark brown eyes.

Mia's heart thudded. "I'm just glad I'm in isolation with you and the kitties," she murmured. "If I'd been all by my lonesome in the new place during this, I would've gone out of my mind."

In the distance, a dog barking echoed through the air, and the hickory trees along the way swayed. All around them, the office buildings towered, casting long, narrow shadows onto the asphalt. Mia's heart lifted, and she walked with an ease she hadn't felt in years.

"You're not joking. Talking to the cats would get old after week one. Besides, there's no one else I'd rather spend a quarantine with," Sky responded, not looking Mia's way. A faint flush coated Sky's cheeks, and Mia licked her lips. God, this woman. Given half the chance, she'd fucking devour her.

"Back atcha, beautiful," Mia responded. They turned onto another street, and the first hints of green peeked through at the end of the block. "Besides, I'm the lucky one here getting to eat all of the fantastic cuisine you make. Holy hell, I think I could eat cassoulet every day for the rest of my life."

"Hey, I've got to put my culinary training to use while I'm temporarily unemployed," Sky said with a shrug, even though a small, satisfied smile played on her lips. "Can't lose my edge."

Sky slowed her pace the closer they got to Cool Springs Park, and Mia took the opportunity to match her steps. She slid her palm against Sky's, threading her fingers through. They hadn't discussed what was going on between them yet, but she'd held hands with Sky far before they'd ever locked lips.

Sky glanced to her, the warmth in those eyes radiating through her. The woman had a soft, sturdiness to her features, like the trees that grew around them, roots solidly planted in the earth. Mia grinned back and swung their arms like Sky had been doing on their walk over. Unlike when they were kids, though, she could feel the buzzing in the air between them, a delicious tension she wanted to sink her teeth into. She didn't miss how they both continued to steal glances like gasps of breath.

The black gates of Cold Springs Park rose in the distance, but they headed in on the opposite side. To her right lay the Barbie-doll houses lining this section of town, each one exactly the same, and to her left, those green lawns sprawled out with the first vibrant hints of early spring, daffodils, wild violets, and buds on the bushes beckoning. Mia squeezed Sky's hand as they got closer.

"Well damn, I haven't been here in years," Mia said, watching the spray of the fountain. The sun sparkled off the droplets of water, causing her heart to skip a note.

"You were off being a hotshot in Seattle," Sky teased, even though Mia noticed the cautious edge to her joke.

She'd been so anxious to get out of living with her mother that she'd chosen the furthest state away, but she never stopped and thought about how her move might've affected Sky. Mia tucked the bit of self-flagellation away for another day. Right now, she just needed to enjoy the sunlight and the fresh air.

Mia cast her a sidelong glance. "Seattle's got an abundance of rain and good coffee," she responded. "Nothing to make me a hotshot. I gathered myself the grandest collection of phony friends who pretty much made me want to avoid hipsters like the plague."

"Good luck," Sky said. "One step into Philly and you're flooded with them."

"God, I missed the East Coast," Mia said as they strode past the green fields sprawling out on either side of them, dandelions swaying in the breezes. "First thing I'm doing when the weather gets nice out and this whole quarantine thing lifts is drive to Rehoboth, even if I just go for the day."

The spindly trees stretched high toward the achingly blue sky, the first buds of color beginning to grow on their branches. In the near distance, she could hear the splash from the fountain, the sound coursing through her.

"Rehoboth is still a fantastic fucking beach. The gay scene's great there," Sky responded. "Aubs, Kyle, and I always go down for a weekend in the summer. We've been doing our beach trip for years now." She cast a hesitant glance her way. "If you want, you could join us this year."

Mia didn't bother restraining her grin. Whenever Sky mentioned Aubrey, she got the slightest stir of jealousy she had no right to feel. After all, Aubrey had been there for Sky when Mia hadn't, and she couldn't begrudge Sky that closeness. But goddamn, she regretted leaving every time she heard stories of Sky, Aubrey, and their friend Kyle's adventures—ones Mia should've been there for.

"I'd love to go with you guys," Mia responded. Truth be told, she wanted to go as Sky's girlfriend. They made their way closer to the fountain, past the pillars with the slatted overhang. They walked over to the small tan fencing surrounding the bricked over-look. Mia rested her hand on the cool surface of the fence in front of her, the bit of chill bracing her.

She needed to figure her life out before she started making promises. While she didn't have plans of moving away again, she also didn't have anything attaching her to this place apart from Sky. When she'd stayed in Seattle after college, she'd remained for Derek, and she couldn't bring herself to do that again.

Her elbow bumped against Sky's, which directed her attention back to the gorgeous woman by her side.

She could feel Sky's heated gaze, and when Mia turned to face her, the sight of the woman sent her careening all over again. The sun brought out the rich golden tones in her brown hair and highlighted the even color of her tanned skin. Those full lips beck-oned, lush and inviting. With her so close, she didn't stand a chance.

Mia leaned in, closing the distance between them.

This wasn't the kiss from the other night, filled with exploration and desperation. No, this was sanguine and slow as she caressed Sky's lips, tasting her, all coffee and mint. Sky's palms settled around her hips with a weight that suspended her in place even as they kissed with a pristine sweetness, like the first bite into an apple.

The sun beat down on her shoulders, but the heat didn't come close to the lazy, golden sort flowing through her in the wake of this kiss. She twined her arms around Sky's shoulders, sinking into the steady grip of this woman, the one thing keeping her from floating off. The crisp scent of the water traveled her way, cool breezes coating her skin.

Mia drank it all in, the soft whistle of the wind, the gentle breaths as Sky pulled back only to return for more, and the heat that flared between their bodies.

All of the worries and concerns from before melted away in the wake of this beautiful spring day and this fever-sweet kiss.

One day at a time.

CHAPTER NINE

After the scorching make-out session under the sunshine at the park earlier, Sky's core thrummed. Every time she glanced over to Mia, she needed to pinch herself in disbelief that this might be happening. As much as her libido wanted to push things further, she couldn't bring herself to take the lead.

Not like Mia needed any help in that department, though. The woman was as direct and bold as she'd always been, nothing like the way Sky cowered behind the ever-expanding wall of her fears.

Sky leaned against the couch, her legs sprawled out. Mia was taking a shower, which had her mind wandering for the thousandth time to what the hot as hell woman would look like naked. The sound of the streaming water shut off, and Sky bit her lower lip, trying to exorcise the images running rampant through her mind.

No matter how much her heart wanted to take a leap, she could feel Mia restraining herself, not offering every last thought that bubbled up in her mind the way she always used to. Sky didn't know what to make of the change, whether something had happened in their time apart, or if Mia was holding back because she just wanted a fling.

Sky was too damn scared to ask.

She could barely believe they'd kissed. She'd spent her entire high school career indulging in fantasies of Mia looking at her with the same silken threads of longing she'd found herself spiderwebbed in. Outside her windows, the sun had begun to set, lowering past the horizon line. Sky rolled onto her feet and paused at the window as she passed, her fingertips resting on the surface of the glass. The gold, amber, and crimson streaks caused her throat to catch.

She should love sunsets—the colors were blindingly beautiful, and the soft gravity in the air at this time of evening held her in thrall. However, all the sunset did was remind her of endings.

And she'd faced too many to want the reminder.

Sky wandered to the opposite side of her living room where she kept her bar cabinet. She cracked the doors open. While she and Mia tipped back the occasional glass of wine or bottle of beer, they hadn't gotten into the hard liquor. However, she hadn't forgotten Mia's request early on to dive into the deep stuff of what happened in their time apart.

She pulled out the Jack Daniels.

Sky's door creaked open, and Mia stepped out. Her attached bathroom had a bath and shower combo, yet her mind plummeted to filthy thoughts at the idea of Mia in her bedroom. Her friend's hair hung in wet waves down to her shoulders, and she wore a thin tank top that may as well have exposed her tits as well as a loose pair of yoga pants. Knowing what a fucking tease this woman had become, she guaranteed Mia dressed that way on purpose.

Sky took a seat on one side of the futon and patted the space in front of her. "I know you wanted the catch-up talk, so here's the Jack, babe." She nudged the bottle on the floor beside her.

Mia's grin widened, her blue eyes glittering like the sun over the waves. "Skylar Jenkins volunteering emotional talks? It's my lucky day."

"The alcohol's involved for a reason," Sky

responded, her tone teasing even though she hadn't been kidding. Every time she talked about the past, especially about her junior year, her skin felt like she'd poured bleach over a sunburn. Her lack of opening up had been one of the main stumbling blocks with every girlfriend of hers. Yet asking Mia to pour her heart out with no return wasn't fair. She knew that.

And she wanted to know what happened between Mia and Derek, how things had ended, how their time apart had changed her. She needed to know if this was a rebound fling or if they stood the chance at something real.

Although, if she were honest, she'd become such a pro at self-sabotage, she'd ruin things anyway. Every new relationship, every attachment reminded her of how fast they could get snatched away from her.

And so, she'd distanced before they could leave her.

Ace move on her part.

Mia sat beside her, moving close enough for their thighs to touch. If that wasn't distracting, she didn't know what was. Sky unscrewed the bottle of Jack and took a swig. The sharp, rich taste of the whiskey coursed down her throat, warming her from the inside out. Mia smelled like peaches, post-shower making the scent even stronger. Sky wanted to taste her so badly. She squeezed her thighs together instead, trying to ignore her pulsing need.

"So, I guess this is the exes talk, right?" Mia asked, casting a glance her way. "Feels like we got this a bit backward. Isn't the dating history nonsense brought up on the first date?"

"Well, we never had that sort of thing," Sky murmured, not sure what to say.

"Though I guess we'd have to be dating to follow the rules," Mia said, tipping her head to the side. Sky's heart squeezed tight. This was where she should jump in and make some claim, especially with the curious, searching look in Mia's eyes. When Sky failed to respond, Mia sucked in a sharp breath. "No pressure. I don't know where you are, but I've got a lot to sort through with starting my life all over again. Probably not the time to enter a serious relationship."

Even though Sky pretty much pushed Mia into the response, she couldn't help the sharp sting in her heart when Mia said the words aloud. Still, she couldn't deny what she wanted right now. "I'm the last person who's going to put pressure on you," Sky said. "We're stuck in the same house for the next two weeks, potentially the next month, so let's agree to toss complications by the wayside—no promises right now."

Even as she said the words, they felt wooden on her tongue. Mia tensed for a moment but let out a hiss of breath.

"No promises, no pressure—is that our motto now?" Mia said, her voice soft in an attempt to tease. Sky wished she could read the woman's thoughts to try and gauge how she felt. Sky never questioned Mia cared, but if she fell for her best friend only for everything to disintegrate, they might as well pronounce her dead on the spot, because her heart wouldn't survive.

Sky took another swig of Jack before passing the bottle over to Mia. "If we're going to survive this quarantine, probably." The whiskey had begun to warm her cheeks enough that she could talk about other things. If she continued down this trail, she'd end up confessing her undying love for Mia Brownstone and send the woman running. "So, what did you want to know, Mia B? I'm an open book."

Mia snorted. "We both know that's not true. You'll talk after much pushing and coercion. But let's dive into exes. When did your last relationship end?" Mia shifted in her seat to lean back, laying her head on Sky's thighs. She wished she'd worn more than running shorts and a loose tee, because the skin-to-skin contact short-circuited her brain.

Sky chewed on her lip as she contemplated Mia's question. "Last girlfriend was Ally Sedonis. We met at the bar. Aubs introduced us because she wanted to chat up Ally's best friend. We ended up sitting back and watching Aubs flirt her way into Ally's friend's pants and cracked jokes. At the end of the night, we swapped numbers, and things went from there."

"Sounds like the perfect meet-cute," Mia commented, stretching her arms overhead. The motion placed her breasts front and center, which became harder and harder to ignore. Mia's voice had taken a slight edge to it, and again, Sky questioned if a hint of jealousy rang in her tone.

Sky shrugged. "Lasted for close to a year, and then six months ago, Ally decided I wasn't adventurous enough for her. Not like I could blame her. I work a lot and my hours aren't anyone's preference."

"That's some bullshit," Mia responded, glancing at her. "You're plenty adventurous."

"Not for a chick who wanted to go out with friends all the time or hit the clubs," Sky said. "Besides, the second the relationship required more effort, I started throwing myself into work more. Aubs says I self-sabotage like a champion."

"Why?" Mia's gaze burned into her.

Sky swallowed hard and stared at the ceiling. She'd promised Mia this conversation, even though she knew they'd be taking the mandoline and paring past the surface tonight. Sky reached down and took another swig from the whiskey to focus on a different sort of burn than the one behind her eyes. "I know the drill by now. Everyone leaves."

Mia's eyes widened, and she reached up, her fingertips brushing along the side of Sky's chin. "I'm sorry, beautiful."

Sky shrugged, trying to ignore the sting of the tears. Mia had been her best friend on this planet, and when she'd ditched for college, the absence had nearly broken her. But Jamie—that was the permanent one. That was the one that destroyed her first. "Not just you, babe. I picked up some shitty curse along the way."

"If you're cursed, I'll eat my shirt," Mia responded.

Sky snorted. "I'm not sure you want to do that—though I'm not going to lie, I appreciate the view."

Mia's fingers rested along Sky's chin, and she brushed a thumb along her lip. Christ, if this woman didn't stop with the sweet affection, she'd be bawling in seconds. Sky broke away to snag the liquor and tipped back another swig of Jack.

"Your turn. What was the deal with you and Derek?" Sky asked, doing her best to hold back the way her eyes watered. Mia had always been a safe place, which was the sole reason she'd agreed to do this opening up thing in the first place. Sky wrapped her hand around Mia's slender waist, her arm resting over the woman's stomach.

Mia rolled her eyes. "We ended up in the same group of friends and clicked. And things were brilliant at first. I know it sounds stupid, but I've been wanting to settle down since high school. Probably just to spite my mom, if I'm being honest. And with Derek? He seemed like the whole package—funny, talented, and serious about the relationship."

"What happened?" Sky asked, squeezing Mia's side.

Mia's gaze darkened. "Apparently I'm too needy. He started pulling away after we graduated and moved in together, and then one day, bam—break up. There was no pre-empt, but from what I've heard in our friend group, he'd gotten cold feet about committing so early on." She met Sky's eyes. "Who knows? Maybe I'm the fool, and Mom's right."

Sky shook her head. "Fuck no. Your mother is never right, Mia B."

Mia let out a short, acerbic laugh.

The idea of that sort of commitment with Mia, of

this turning into something serious terrified her. She wanted the real deal with Mia, more than she'd wanted anything in her life. But losing someone who'd ingrained on her so deeply? Jamie's death ruined her, and she still hadn't stitched all of her ragged scraps together again.

If she let this connection between her and Mia flare into the relationship she wanted? Fuck, she couldn't imagine the wreckage of twisted metal and shards if their roller coaster flew off the tracks.

"Don't let your mom get in your head," Sky said, her voice softening. "Derek was fucking crazy to give you up, but I can't say I'm not a little happy about it. If the two of you hadn't broken up, you would've never come back here. And if I can pull one beautiful thing out of all the chaos our world's in, it's you."

Mia's cheeks pinked. Her gaze deepened with a desire that coursed through Sky. The headiness felt better than the whiskey she'd tipped back.

Mia pushed up from lying on her lap to turn and face her. "You're not drunk, are you?" she asked, her gaze seeking as she tried to assess Sky's sobriety.

"Just a little warm, but I'm clear-headed," Sky responded, unable to look away from Mia's gaze.

Mia slipped her hand beneath Sky's shirt, her palm resting on her bare skin. Sky sucked in a sharp breath.

The look in Mia's eyes turned predatory, a focus there that pinned her in place.

A look like that and Sky would offer everything she had to give.

"Good," Mia purred. "Because I want to taste you tonight."

CHAPTER TEN

Mia had wanted to plunge headfirst into talking about their exes, the emotional shit she normally adored.

Except, when Sky had been speaking about her ex, all she could think of was how they'd agreed to keep things light and easy. How Sky had been willing to slap the label girlfriend on these other women, but the second they'd kissed, she'd bolted, and even now, Mia needed to handle her like a blown glass ornament.

It pissed her off a little.

Jealousy scorched her veins, making her feel more possessive than she had in years. Her hand pressed against Sky's bare skin, the heat and softness making her delirious. Sky might have become the queen of self-sabotage in her relationships, but Mia refused to let the woman push her away.

Even if she needed to play her best friend's games to get past those walls.

Mia slid her hand down to reach for the hem of Sky's shirt. She glanced up to meet Sky's eyes, tilting her head in question. Sky nodded, those umber eyes drenched with desire. Mia's heart fluttered at the depth of that look. She'd felt like an idiot for missing the clues throughout the years of Sky's attraction, but now that the light had flickered on… damn. The woman had a way of making her feel like no one else existed.

Honestly, she'd been craving that singular attention more than she would admit. She just wanted someone to look at her like she mattered, like she could be as important in their eyes as they were in hers.

Mia grabbed the hem of Sky's T-shirt and lifted the worn fabric up and over. She bit back a groan once she tossed it to the ground. Thank fuck this woman never wore a bra. Her tanned skin gleamed in the dim lighting of her living room, and her tits looked goddamn delicious, perfect globes with darker areolas. The way her ink framed either arm amplified the smooth canvas of her skin that Mia was dying to taste.

She couldn't help but notice the words tattooed around her side "Do I Dare Disturb the Universe?" the line so perfect for Skylar Jenkins.

Mia pressed her fingers right in the center of Sky's chest to give the woman a light push against the futon.

Sky collapsed back, her chest heaving with every breath.

Fucking mesmerizing.

Mia hovered over her to press a kiss to her lips. The moment she leaned down and Sky's nipples brushed against the thin fabric of her shirt, her desperation to devour this woman grew. Sky tasted like whiskey, sharp and smoky, and Mia couldn't help but draw another kiss from her lips before she traveled down to scrape her teeth along the side of Sky's neck.

Sky let out a guttural moan, her hands settling around Mia's waist. She loved how responsive Sky was to every single touch, how this woman stared at her with a starry-sky yearning that made her somehow feel whole again. Mia nipped and sucked her way down Sky's neck, brushing her lips against her collarbone as she reached out to circle a hand around one of her breasts. The firm weight of them, velvet to the touch, caused Mia to squeeze her thighs tighter.

She'd grown impossibly wet once she took Sky's shirt off, and the pressure continued increasing the lower she traveled.

Mia leaned in to lick the tip of Sky's nipple. Sky ground her hips against hers, and Mia's grin widened.

"Damn, you're a fantasy come to life," Sky murmured, her voice a hoarse scrape.

Mia's heart squeezed tight. "That's my line, beautiful. I could spend hours on your tits alone." However, she was nothing if not determined. She let go of Sky's breast and continued to prowl down the length of her torso, pressing kisses and nips along the way. Each time, Sky thrust her hips against her, reminding her of the eventual goal.

"Lucky for you, I'm not too sadistic," Mia murmured between bites. Her core ached, and wetness pooled between her legs from how damn slick her pussy had become. The exploration of this woman's body turned her on so unbelievably bad. "And I've been wanting to taste you from the moment I stepped into this apartment."

"Fuck, babe," Sky moaned, her eyes closed, head tilted back. "Are you trying to give me an aneurysm? Who's this dirty-talking stranger and where did my Mia go?"

The "my" stuck out in Mia's mind, causing her pulse to quicken. If only.

"Darling, you might know me better than most, but you've never been on the receiving end of this side," she murmured, brushing her lips closer and closer to those beautiful hipbones. "God, I bet your pussy tastes glorious," she continued between kisses and bites. Sky's legs opened on instinct, and the woman's throat fluttered with the desperate breaths coming from her.

"I'm not going to lie. You just as much as whisper on my clit, and I'm liable to come," Sky breathed out. "I've never been this turned on in my life."

"Me neither," Mia responded, her voice deepening a notch. She wasn't lying. She'd never experienced chemistry like this before. Confidence thrummed through her veins with Sky, because the woman always lifted her up, and the heady combination of this unearthed attraction with the safety of her best friend created one hell of a drug.

"Last chance to back out," Mia murmured, hooking her fingers on the waistband of Sky's shorts.

Sky's breath hitched. "When have I ever backed out of a game of chicken?"

The corners of Mia's lips turned up. "Never. Don't say I didn't give you a warning."

Knees digging into the futon, Mia slid the elastic of

Sky's shorts and panties down her hips, desperate to see more of this beautiful woman. Sky assisted in shifting her legs until the cumbersome clothing pooled on the floor beside them.

Mia had never seen Sky stark naked before, no matter how many times they'd slept over at each other's houses in high school. How the fuck had she spent all those years missing out on this? They could've indulged in an entirely different sort of sleep-over the whole time.

Mia soaked in the sight of Sky, from her tanned, smooth skin to the stark curve of her hips. She wanted those muscular thighs wrapped around her. Sky always hated her broad-shouldered frame back in high school but seeing the woman flush out before her like this was unbearably sexy. The way her thick brown hair parted to the side, the longer ends barely coming down to her ear and how those deep chestnut eyes shone with an intensity Mia had been searching years for—Mia was going to devour her.

"I think it's a little unfair that I'm stripped down and you haven't taken a thing off," Sky grumbled, a flush staining her cheeks as she glanced away.

Mia climbed over her and tilted Sky's chin back in her direction to plant a kiss on those lush lips. "Hush, beautiful. You'll have your turn. Let me enjoy you right now."

Sky might not be in the place to talk out her feelings or even confront this connection that had always existed between them, exposed to the light at last. If she couldn't voice it, then Mia would show her.

Sky's throat bobbed as she swallowed, but she offered a nod. Mia settled between her legs. Sky was trimmed, her dark curls moist with a slickness Mia couldn't wait to lick up. The musky scent made her desperate to taste. Sky's legs fell open, and Mia settled between them, running her fingertips across those muscular thighs.

She lowered her mouth to the enticing soaked folds and let out a light exhale. Sky shuddered in response. They'd reached the point of no return—once they crossed this line, they couldn't backtrack to anything innocent or simple between them. Worries and anxieties had threatened to crowd her out earlier, but right now, lust scorched through any of those thoughts.

Mia might've made a lot of mistakes along the way, but she'd only moved forward by taking chances.

She licked between Sky's folds, and the woman let out a low moan, deep and guttural. Mia found the soft nub of Sky's clit and hummed against the sensitive spot, enjoying how she tilted her hips up as if she begged for more. Mia gripped Sky's thighs and began to lick at her clit in slow, deliberate strokes. Sky tasted tart and sweet, and Mia couldn't help but draw out each lick just to watch the woman writhe.

Every time Sky bucked her hips, Mia lapped at her clit over and over again. She needed to squeeze her thighs tighter from the way her pussy was a violin string ready to pluck just from watching Sky's reactions. The woman's breaths came out in short pants, and the flush across her cheeks was a brush of the sunrise. Sky's heat surrounded her along with those solid thighs, and as she knelt before her, licking and sucking at her clit, her own panties had grown so soaked she'd have to wring them out.

Mia drove the point of her tongue inside Sky, enjoying the explosive moans coming from her, husky and breathy in a way that made Mia hotter than ever.

"Don't stop," Sky murmured, her hips shifting to the same rhythm that Mia drove into her. Mia reached up and brushed her thumb across Sky's clit. The woman's legs trembled, droplets of sweat beading on them. She hadn't been lying—she was close.

Mia sucked in a breath and drove her tongue back in, circling her thumb across Sky's clit until her legs full out shook in response. Mia lost herself in the inexorable heat, the throb between her legs, and the feel of Sky's thighs pressing in closer as the woman's hips lifted again. The breath hitched in Sky's throat.

Mia pulled her tongue out to drag the tip over the woman's sensitive clit, relishing in the way she trembled before her. Sky's moans were a seductive music, and she continued lapping away at her clit, finding a slow, deliberate rhythm. She licked down one more time as Sky's breath snagged in her throat again, and the woman's thighs clamped around her. Sky's entire body quaked in the wake of her orgasm.

Mia continued sucking and licking at her clit until Sky's breaths evened and her hips lowered. She pressed a kiss on the inside of Sky's thigh and then bit the thick muscle there. God, she was so turned on her vision grew fuzzy. Sky reached down and threaded her fingers through Mia's hair, the touch to her scalp sending a shiver down her spine.

"Goddamn, woman," Sky murmured, beginning to push herself up. "That was… unbelievable." Her tender look stopped Mia still, even as she'd lifted her arm to wipe off her mouth. "I didn't think you could look sexier, but your hair tousled like that and my juices glistening on your lips…." Sky tilted back her head for a moment, letting out a guttural noise before she leaned forward to kiss her.

Mia sank into the kiss, desperate for more, for some sort of release to the mounting pressure inside her. She slipped her tongue into Sky's mouth, deepening it, and the woman let out another moan that thrummed between them.

Sky pulled back. "I could kiss you for the rest of my life and never get enough, but right now, there were promises made. It's my turn."

Mia's mind reeled at the words coming from Sky, feeding those deep desires for something longer than a temporary arrangement. Before she could process, Sky's fingers drifted to the hem of Mia's tank top, lifting it up and over.

"You have no idea how badly I wanted to peel this off you," Sky murmured, running her palms up and down Mia's bare waist.

Mia's lips quirked into a half-smile. "I had a little bit of an idea."

"You're a damn minx," Sky responded, shaking her head. Mia's nipples pebbled, and as Sky drifted her thumbs across them, cupping her breasts in each hand, she couldn't help the desperate noise bubbling in the back of her throat. A soft grin played on Sky's lips. "Don't think I missed the way you've been flaunting those beautiful tits around the house. I've noticed. Every. Single. Time."

Mia swallowed hard. The intensity in Sky's voice fulfilled everything she'd craved. She'd never met anyone with such a singular focus in her life. From the moment they'd kissed, the chemistry exploding between them, she'd been fantasizing about what it'd be like to be devoured by someone with that attention and dedication.

Fuck.

Sky's palms slid along her waist, and she shimmied Mia's yoga pants down her thighs. "I'm sorry, but I can't wait."

"No apology necessary," Mia responded, her voice coming out faint. Sky's dirty talk was just like her—this wonderous, explorative thing. As Sky tugged Mia's yoga pants and underwear off, tossing them to the ground, Sky sucked in a sharp breath. They were both bare on this futon. She couldn't do anything but watch as Sky rose to sit on her legs and gripped the inside of Mia's thigh. The touch was firm, sure, and Mia rested back on her elbows, watching what the woman might do next.

"I've wanted to taste you longer than you could know," Sky murmured, the words coming out so soft she almost missed them. Her heart wrenched tight at the idea of all those wasted years.

"I'm here now," Mia responded, reaching up to trail her fingers along Sky's chin.

"Don't I fucking know it," Sky said, drawing Mia's one leg up and over her shoulder. She crouched lower, and Mia let go of her face, sinking all the way onto her back. Her knee rested on Sky's shoulder, her heel on her back, and Sky brought her mouth down to close the distance.

Sky's lips fluttered across her folds, and a whole-body shiver rocked through her. She needed this bad enough to beg, and she opened her mouth, prepared to when Sky's tongue came out to play. The woman didn't bother with teasing or slow seduction. The angle of Mia's leg wrapped over Sky's shoulder opened her wide, pussy exposed as the woman licked and sucked at her clit with a laser focus.

The breath knocked out of her lungs, and her fingers curled into the futon on either side of her as she succumbed to the onslaught of sensations. Sky gripped one hand around Mia's thigh, the other wrapping to cup her ass, controlling the angle the entire time as she devoured her with a precision Mia should've expected.

Most of the time, she took ages to come and sometimes didn't at all, based on the partner, but the build-up had her sensitized and panting. Sky's plush lips, how she sucked and lapped into her, caused that pleasure to grow to the point where she could only focus on the woman before her. She looked so goddamn sexy tucked between her legs, her short chestnut strands sweeping over her forehead.

Sky's demanding rhythm had Mia's breath catching in her throat and sweat beading across her forehead. Her back stuck to the fabric of the futon. Each lick across her clit brought sparks, and the tightness that seemed too much to bear grew impossible. All she could smell was sweat, sex, and the woodsy scent of her best friend.

Mia's breaths came out shallow, and she closed her eyes, surrendering to the bliss rolling through her at every stroke. With this perfect angle, her heel dug into Sky's back each time the woman brought her closer. Sky didn't slow, increasing the force as she pushed her to the brink. Intensity mounted to the point she couldn't stand it anymore, but even as her hips tried to thrust up, Sky's grip remained tight, the woman keeping her in place.

Mia's legs tensed as Sky sucked her clit again, the pressure reaching the limit.

Her clit fluttered, and the sensation began to crest as her entire body quaked. Sky gripped her even tighter, not letting go when she came. Mia's eyes rolled back in her head, her breath snagging, and the sweat beading along her forehead as she careened. The orgasm swept through, and she curled forward, her mind blanking and pleasure soaking her like the first dip into a hot bath.

Mia began to come back to earth, satiation melting her body into the futon. Sky lowered Mia's leg to the floor, completely jelly right now in the wake of that orgasm.

"Holy hell, beautiful," Mia murmured, reaching up to beckon Sky down with her. "Please tell me I don't have to bother with moving at all tonight."

Sky shook her head. "This is where I grab a blanket." Sky paused to snag one from the floor and bring it over the both of them. "And we throw something on Netflix and cuddle."

"You mean we could've been having mind-blowing sex and naked cuddles this entire time?" Mia pouted. "We've been missing out."

"Well, we'll make up for it," Sky said, settling in behind her and wrapping an arm around her shoulders.

Mia nestled against her, loving the way they fit together. Her entire body flushed from the orgasm and her dizzied mind still hadn't returned to earth, but she wasn't sure if it was going to. If anything solidified the rising feelings she'd been questioning over Skylar Jenkins, this had.

For a few blissful moments, she shut off her brain, pressed against Sky, and pretended this was something she could keep.

CHAPTER ELEVEN

THEY ALREADY PASSED THE TWO-WEEK MARK FOR THIS quarantine, but Delaware's government extended the shelter-in-place ruling another month. Having Mia by her side made all the difference. She continued cooking the meals while Mia worked during the week. At night, Mia curled up beside her in bed, and she'd honestly never slept so well.

Sky stood in her kitchen, the sliding door to her balcony open to let the honeysuckle breeze in. Shelley and Byron loved to prowl out there and had been basking under sunbeams from the moment she opened it up.

Sky leaned against the counter as she chopped up some fresh tomato and iceberg lettuce, the bacon crisping on the skillet beside her. Mia would be breaking for lunch any minute, and she wanted to have something prepared. She'd tried to delude herself that having sex would've diminished her fantasies for the woman, but that route never seemed to work.

If anything, she wanted Mia more than ever now. After experiencing the blissful way their bodies connected, she couldn't imagine heading out in the dating cesspool. Like any Tinder date could compare to Mia Brownstone. Lucky for her, Mia had become just as insatiable, which meant long, late hours of lazy fucking and then waking up to that gorgeous woman still in her arms. Being with Mia was all she'd ever dreamed of, a joy so exquisite her heart hurt with how much she wanted more and more of this.

Sky smeared the mayo on the inside of the bread and finished assembling two BLT sandwiches right as her phone rang.

She glanced at the screen, frowning at the number. It wasn't programmed in, but she recognized it.

"Mrs. Brownstone?" Sky asked as she picked up. The only reason she remembered the number was because the woman hadn't changed her cell from back in high school, and she'd called her plenty of times asking for Mia.

"Sky, it's good to hear your voice," Mrs. Brownstone said, even as her words leeched the warmth from the room. "I couldn't get ahold of Mia, and I know she's staying with you, so I figured I would try your phone instead."

"Ah, yeah, Mia's in the middle of IT calls at work," Sky explained, leaning against her counter. "Need me to pass along a message?"

"I do. I'll be out with Jared the rest of the day making arrangements and won't have time for a call then."

Sky rolled her eyes, grateful for the distance of the phone. She didn't know how Mia dealt with this frigid woman all these years. Everything was on her terms or not at all.

"Jared's work situation has shifted with the quarantine. Once this is all over, they want him to move to Texas as soon as possible for a promoted position, and he's asked me to join him." Mrs. Brownstone delivered the news in a cool, crisp way. Sky's stomach dropped out.

Sky couldn't get over the news—Mia and her mother had lived here their entire lives. But, what reason would Mia have to stay if her mother was leaving? "I'm guessing you're considering going?"

"I've always wanted to venture out somewhere else. Mia will understand. She can come visit me in Austin, and we'll get to see the sights."

No, Mia wouldn't understand. She tried so hard with her brittle mother, who only gave a damn about herself. In that moment, Sky hated Mia's mom more than ever.

"Right," Sky said through gritted teeth. "Anything else?"

"Not that I can think of. Thanks for passing along the message, dear," Mrs. Brownstone said, and with that, she hung up.

Sky sagged against the counter. Great, now she had to break the news. Mia's mom was such a raging asshole. The cats had begun to stir from their stupor under the sunbeams at the scent of the bacon, and their chorus of meowls sounded a second later. She would have to put Mia's sandwich somewhere safe from her little critters.

The door to her side room swung open. *Dammit.*

Mia stepped out, stretching her arms over her head, her phone in hand. "Finally, break time."

"I made lunch," Sky said, placing one of the BLTs on the breakfast nook.

Mia took a seat at the stool. "You're a fucking miracle, you know that?" Her nose wrinkled as she looked down at her phone. "Looks like I missed three calls from Mom. I'll have to call her back before break ends."

Sky glanced up. "Did you know the scientific name for brain freeze is sphenopalatine ganglioneuralgia?" She took a bite of the BLT to cover up the awkward blurt. Her focus switched to the burst of flavors of salt from the bacon, of crispness from the lettuce and tomato mingling on her tongue with the creamy mayo. When she glanced up, Mia gave her a pointed look.

"You only start spouting rando facts when you're uncomfortable. Spill." Mia took a few bites from the BLT even though her gaze never left Sky, which was a stunning feat.

Sky skimmed fingers through her hair. "When your mom couldn't get ahold of you, she called me instead."

Mia's face fell. "Let me guess—not good news. Is she okay?" The hint of panic in Mia's voice twisted Sky's insides. She hated when this woman hurt.

"She's fine," Sky reassured. "But her boyfriend—Jason, Jared, or whatever—his work is relocating him to Austin, Texas." Sky sucked in a breath, not wanting to broach the next part out loud.

Mia shook her head, and her lips pressed together in a white line. "Let me guess. Mom's moving with him." Her voice turned brittle, but Sky knew Mia was a fraction away from cracking. Despite the way she and her mother butted heads for years, Mia never stopped trying with that woman, even when Mrs. Brownstone didn't deserve the attempts.

Sky offered a helpless shrug. "She wanted me to pass along the message because she'll be out the rest of the day." The admission coated her tongue like bile, as if she were somehow complicit with Mia's mother's bullshit.

"Sounds just like her," Mia responded, pushing up from her seat to pour herself another cup of coffee. Her hands trembled as she spooned sugar into the cup. Sky ran fingers through her hair again on reflex. Did she reach out to comfort or let her continue? Mia made the choice for her. "Go figure, I finally move back to the area and Mom finds an excuse to ditch. And she didn't even have the guts to tell me herself, making you do the dirty work instead. Just fucking like her."

"I'm sorry," Sky murmured, hating to see her like this.

Mia reached over to brush her fingertips under Sky's chin, lifting it so their eyes were level. "You have nothing to apologize for, beautiful."

Sky didn't have to question what to do next—she knew Mia better than anyone. She opened her arms wide, and Mia threw herself into the embrace. Sky wrapped her arms tight around her best friend as Mia pressed against her, fingers curling into the fabric of her shirt. Her shoulders trembled, but she wasn't crying. Still, her breaths evened while they pressed together like this. Sky rested her chin on top of Mia's head, grateful for the height difference between them.

"Your mom's such a fuckface," Sky muttered, squeezing Mia tighter. Mia snorted in response.

A rustle sounded beside them, and Sky glanced over to spot Byron on the countertop, trying to tug a piece of bacon from her sandwich.

"Crap," Sky said, letting go of Mia to reach out and swat Byron away. He leapt to the ground, piece of bacon in tow, and her sandwich had gotten torn apart in the process. "Speaking of fuckfaces…."

Mia squeezed Sky's shoulder with a half-smile. "We should know better than to leave food unattended around the vultures. And you're not wrong. My mom is shitty. I don't know why I keep going back expecting a different response from the woman."

Sky shrugged, reassembling her sandwich before Shelley could get any ideas. Mia snagged hers as well, taking a bite.

"She's your mom, babe," Sky said, turning to face her again. "Of course, you're going to try again, and again, and again. She's the only family you've got."

"Can't your mom adopt me?" Mia asked, raising the age-old question she'd asked through high school every time she and her mother were fighting again. "The main reason I went to college so far away was to get a break from the constant tension between me and Mom."

"You know my folks adore you," Sky said, leaning against Mia as they munched on their sandwiches. She'd almost forgotten what having this much physical contact felt like. Even with her past girlfriends, there was never this much. Yet when Mia was around, even as friends, touch had been a constant—holding hands, brushing against each other, leaning on each other, and hugging. Now that they'd started sleeping together, her hunger for touch had grown insatiable, like it'd been reawakened from a long slumber.

She couldn't imagine what would happen when Mia left.

"Let me guess. She also expects me to be the one flying out to visit her when she moves?" Mia asked, the bitterness in her voice corrosive. "Not like she came to see me once when I lived in Seattle."

Sky bobbed her head. "You called it. Ice Queen is pulling her usual MO." She finished off the last bites of her BLT and placed the plate in the dishwasher. Mia snuck by her to drop her plate off as well, their hands brushing together in the process.

Sky chewed on her lip. In the past she would've never comforted Mia this way—but things had changed between them. Before Mia could step away, Sky grabbed her hand and pulled her closer.

Her lips descended over Mia's, and she tasted the salt on her lips as she kissed her. Mia melted into her arms, returning the kiss just as fiercely. Sky swept her tongue inside Mia's mouth, deepening it as she coaxed and caressed with her lips. As fast as the kiss had begun, she pulled away before the desire burning between them got out of hand. Any longer and she'd be tempted to take things further while Mia needed to return to work.

"Well, that was what I needed," Mia murmured, leaning in against Sky. She reached up, rifling her fingers through Sky's short strands, the touch sending a shiver down her spine. "God, I want to keep you."

Sky swallowed hard, panic swirling at her statement. Mia had been who she'd always longed for, and yet she'd become so hardwired to run over the years that she couldn't accept the one woman she wanted most.

"I know, I know," Mia responded, though a string of weariness wove through her words. "Against the rules of light and easy. But you need to know anyway —you're a goddamn catch, Skylar Jenkins."

Sky wanted to speak, but the words just wouldn't flow. Instead, she reached out to grab Mia's hand. "So are you, Mia B. I know your mom moving away has got to hurt, especially with the timing, but you're worth sticking around for."

"Jury's still out on that one," Mia responded with a lopsided grin. "But I've got to get back to work."

"Ice cream and venting tonight?" Sky offered. "We can talk all about your shitty mom being shitty."

Mia's grin widened as she approached the side room. "It's a date." She disappeared behind the door a moment later.

Sky sank against the counter and looked at the ceiling. What the fuck was her damage? Mia defined everything she'd ever wanted in a woman, a lover, a partner.

Except she hadn't been back for a month, and already, their entire situation had been upturned.

She knew what lay at the root of her self-sabotage, but she couldn't go there. The mere idea of returning to those days, those memories, sent her full Medusa, making her skin turn to stone.

Sky hoped she could pull herself together before she fucked this up for good.

CHAPTER TWELVE

MIA STIRRED SUGAR INTO HER CUP OF EARL GREY, enjoying the fragrant steam that wafted her way. Sky sat on the couch, scrolling through her phone listlessly. She'd gotten more erratic as of late, tenser, as if she expected a tripwire around every corner.

Mia had asked her a couple of times if she was okay, to which she got a gruff "Fine" every time. It hadn't been until Mia looked at the calendar and a certain date stuck out—April seventeenth—that she realized what was coming up.

Next week would be the anniversary of Jamie's death.

She'd been around for the one-year anniversary of Sky's sister's death, and those disquieting days wouldn't leave her if she tried. Sky would get more and more withdrawn. After all their time apart, the heavy cloud of depression that descended during these days hadn't changed. Guilt pulsed through her at all of the years she should've reached out to Sky during this month. Instead, she'd gotten so self-involved, so hell-bent on escaping her mom that she'd left Sky behind.

The cool spring air swept in from the balcony, bringing the fresh scent of magnolias and blossoming cherry trees. As much as Sky might want to shut her out, and maybe she deserved the closed door, the woman needed someone right now.

Mia sat on the couch beside her and plucked the phone from Sky's hands.

Sky let out a noise of protest. "What was that for?"

"You've been losing yourself in the thing for the past hour, so why don't you take a break? Grab a blanket. We're going to sit on the balcony and enjoy the beautiful night."

"Maybe I was in the middle of an in-depth conversation," Sky shot back. A second later, she pushed up from her seat. "Or that could be a lie and boredom took over." She glanced at Mia's steaming mug. "If we're sitting outside, I'm grabbing tea too."

"See you out there," Mia said, stopping to snag one of the cozy blankets from the futon. She stepped out onto the concrete balcony, and Shelley and Byron approached to greet her, weaving between her legs. Her hands were too full for pets, but once she set the tea on the small glass table and spread the blanket out, she skimmed her fingers through the fur of Byron who'd come to nestle by her.

Out past the balcony lay a fringe of trees and tall buildings further past, but beyond all of that, the sky was clear, featuring a canopy of stars. The delicate fragrances swept her way, swirling through her like fresh hope, and she couldn't help how her heart lurched as she stared into the distance, all the crystalline light so far away. It reminded her of this dance between her and Sky, powerful, intense, yet untouchable.

Every time she tried to grasp at what this connection between them meant, she found herself scooping up air, and she didn't know how to change that. Mia sucked in a deep breath.

One day at a time.

She'd always been soaring down the highway toward her future at a hundred miles an hour, but where had that gotten her? She'd wasted years with Derek and squandered plenty of friendships back home by throwing her full focus into her Seattle group. The one thing she didn't regret was distance from her mother. Taking the time away from Carol

Brownstone had given Mia a chance to breathe and figure herself out.

Mia took a sip of her tea, the warm liquid rolling through her body like a kiss.

The soft pad of footsteps came from the sliding door, and Sky stepped out, dragging a chenille blanket and holding a mug of tea. Sky paused for a moment to stare ahead of her.

"Damn, it is pretty tonight, though a little colder than I expected." She strode over to where Mia sat, and seconds later, she settled beside her, popping her porcelain mug on the same table. Sky brought the soft blanket around both of their shoulders, and Mia leaned in against her.

"Lucky for me, I've got you to cuddle with," Mia said, snuggling in closer.

Sky wrapped an arm around her with a possessive grip that made Mia's stomach curl with warmth. "Lucky for me, I've got a best friend who knows when I'm sinking and drags me out anyway."

Mia's cheeks flushed. Apparently, she wasn't as crafty as she thought. "Sometimes you just need a little push."

Sky pressed a kiss on the top of her head. "And you've always been the one to give it."

"Remember when we used to go camping in your

backyard?" Mia asked, knowing she kicked right into a subject Sky might recoil from. "You, me, and Jamie would sit there thinking we were so damn cool telling lame-ass horror stories and downing way more sugar than we ever should've. We'd spill out of the cramped tent and spread our sleeping bags on the grass to look up at the stars, just the way they are tonight."

Sky's shoulders tensed, but a soft sigh came from her lips, skating over Mia's skin. "Those were amazing nights. Makes you wish we could go back to them, even for a little bit."

Mia wove her fingers through Sky's, bringing her hand up to press a soft kiss to it. "I miss her," she murmured.

Silence followed, but Mia expected as much. She needed Sky to know, to understand she hadn't forgotten about Jamie. The younger Jenkins sister had been the polar opposite of Sky—all pluck with a bright personality that made the world glitter around you. She'd also been annoyingly optimistic and used to piss them off so bad with her constant series of pranks.

"Fuck, I miss her too," Sky mouthed out at last, her voice hoarse. "Every damn day."

Mia squeezed Sky's hand entwined with hers. "I know I was off being a garbage friend in Seattle, and I should've reached out. But every April, I remembered."

Sky's legs sprawled out around her, and Sky clutched to her like the cords of a parachute mid freefall. Mia nuzzled against her, knowing how much the woman needed the affection right now, even if she'd never ask.

"What do you think Jamie would've thought about this whole arrangement?" Mia asked. Talking about Jamie should've hurt more, but being with Sky and reminiscing like this? All she could remember were those beautiful memories the three of them had shared.

Sky snorted. "The initial response would've been 'ew,' because you were like a sister to her too. No one wants to imagine their sibling getting down and dirty with one of their best friends."

Sky rested her chin on Mia's head, something she'd started doing ever since they'd kissed. Honestly, how right it felt made Mia a little faint around the edges. Mia held onto Sky's arms wrapped around her, basking in the warmth between them and the scent of Sky mingling with the sweet fragrances of a spring night.

"But," Sky continued, her tone dropping an octave, "she would've been thrilled. Jamie was the only one who knew I had a crush on you back in high school."

"God, I wish I hadn't been so blind in high school,"

Mia mumbled. "Who knows what might've happened if we'd gotten together back then. I wouldn't have gone to Seattle, that's for sure."

Sky's thighs surrounded her, reminding her how good bare skin felt pressed against hers. Fuck, she'd become obsessed.

"Maybe we'd be together, or maybe we would've fucked it all up," Sky said. "I might've known I was a lesbian by the ripe age of eleven when every single crush was on another girl, but not everyone figures themselves out as fast. Besides, we weren't in a super gay-friendly school—I was one of the only out kids there, so what other comparisons did you have? Freddie and Jason?"

"Still sucks," Mia muttered, even though her chest stirred at the understanding Sky offered. Honestly, Sky had been nothing but understanding from the moment she returned home, but something had grown off-kilter between them. Like some dam in Sky needed to burst, but the woman had walled off her pain for too many years for even a trickle to push through. "If you're mad about me leaving then, you know I can take the truth, right?"

Sky shrugged. "Ever consider I dropped off for my own reasons? I can't get mad at you unless I'm going to get mad at myself too."

Mia let out a low huff. "You are a stubborn ass, Skylar Jenkins." One day she'd be able to pry out the answers from her best friend.

"Back atcha, Mia B," Sky responded, her voice husky and teasing. That tone always did something to her, a tingle down her spine, like bottled sex.

"Well, I guess we'll have to make up for all our lost time," Mia said, pulling away from Sky to turn around and face her.

Sky sat before her, legs wide open in those basketball shorts that'd be far too easy to pull off. The soft breezes rolling through swept the woman's short hair to the side, and her eyes were the puppy-dog vulnerable that sent Mia tripping head over heels.

Mia approached in front of her on her hands and knees until she slipped her palm beneath Sky's shirt.

"You're insatiable, babe," Sky said, her eyes crinkling at the edges as she let out a laugh. "Up here?"

Mia offered her a half-smile. "Fucking you under the stars on this gorgeous night? I couldn't think of anything better." She met her eyes, her expression turning serious for a moment. "Life's moving on, whether we like it or not, and we've got new memories to make, beautiful."

Sky's features sobered for a moment, and Mia hesitated, worried she'd crossed a line. However, a second later, Sky grabbed the front of her shirt, hauling her forward to meet her lips in a crushing kiss.

I love you. I love you. I love you.

The words bubbled to her lips again and again, but she never managed to get them out. Instead, she sank into Sky's kiss, caressing her with lips, tongue, and teeth, until they lost themselves in one another.

The stars shone overhead in the night sky, silver, remote, and delicate. Yet as she surrendered to the waves of heat and pleasure with Sky, her body floating higher and higher, maybe those distant stars had grown closer than she'd believed after all.

CHAPTER THIRTEEN

SKY STIRRED THE BUTTER ON THE SKILLET, WATCHING the way it browned as she tried to avoid her thoughts.

Her gaze continued to slip to where Mia sat on the couch with her sketchpad out and a furious focus devoted to it. The skritch skritch skritch of her pen to the paper was a comforting sound, one that vaulted Sky to earlier years. She tossed the chopped mushrooms onto the skillet and dropped in the tortellini, the steam kissing her face.

As much as she'd tried to hold herself back throughout this quarantine, the truth was she'd fallen for Mia years ago. She was hopelessly in love with the woman, and that terrified her. A sense of foreboding had been approaching all week and wouldn't be vanishing any time soon. The days before and after the anniversary of Jamie's passing always brought those thunderheads, and rational decisions eluded her.

Still, around Mia, the gaping cavity inside her chest had started to fill, slowly, slowly, and Sky found herself bypassing borders she'd erected to keep others out as if they'd never existed. Aubs and Kyle were the ones who'd managed to knock down her walls in recent years, but her relationship with both of those women was sisterly. Nothing like the chemistry between her and Mia that had her reeling in disbelief. She finished with the mixture in the skillet, the fragrant scents mingling as the timer went off for the tortellini.

"Dinner will be ready soon," Sky called over.

Mia glanced up from her sketchpad. "Crap, I was in some different zone. Let me get plates." Mia's phone buzzed by her side again. She glanced at it, let out a grimace, and shut the ringer off. More and more recently, someone had been messaging her at all hours of the day and night. It was hard to ignore when they shared the same room and bed. Ever since they'd started having sex, Mia vacated the futon to tangle with Sky in the bed every single night.

Mia hopped up from her crouch and made her way over, her fingers covered in ink stains from her project. Sky's heart thudded a little harder at the sight, like they'd reverted back to high school when Mia's hands were constantly covered in them. Every last detail about this woman had her falling.

She poured the tortellini out, and Mia stepped up with dishes. Next, she spooned the contents of the skillet over the plates.

"Damn, this smells fantastic," Mia said, leaning in to get a waft. "I'm getting spoiled living with a chef— it'd be all too easy to get used to this."

"Trust me, I don't cook this much when I'm working full time," Sky said, unable to help the way her heart lurched. Mia kept dropping not-so-subtle hints of wanting more, casually slipping in comments about how she'd never slept so well as she did with Sky, how she could live with her forever. Sky could tell too that the woman's patience stretched thinner and thinner the longer they put off "the talk" with every lingering look, every time her mouth would open and then she'd close it again. How could Sky explain the sole reason she'd been able to stay with her girlfriends in the past was because she hadn't felt this depth of connection with any of them?

Mia carried the laden plates and utensils over to the breakfast nook and took a seat on one of the stools. "Let's have a mild change of scenery," she suggested.

Sky couldn't help her grin. "You mean you're starting to get sick of my tiny-ass apartment? I was there weeks ago, babe. I want to be able to go out to the parks and bars again. This quarantine needs to end."

"Yeah, but once it ends, that means I've got to help Mom pack for her move to Austin," Mia said, chasing a few tortellini around the plate.

The unsaid lingered in the air between them. When the quarantine ended, Mia would be moving into her new house, and neither of them staked any claims—Sky's fault, she knew.

Not like she could think clearly with the anniversary looming over her.

"Hey, you'll still have me," Sky said. Mia might move on and find someone who could actually vocalize what she wanted, but she couldn't pull herself away from this woman again. Even if the end result would hurt.

Mia's grin softened. Her phone buzzed again.

"Okay, Popular Girl, who's blowing up your spot?" Sky asked, taking a bite of the tortellini and mushrooms. It was a simple dinner, but sometimes those could be just as comforting as the complex ones.

Mia blew out a breath. "Derek."

Sky's skin crawled, but she kept a grin plastered on

her face. "Derek, the track star from high school or Derek, the ex-boyfriend?"

Mia shot her a look. "Derek, the ex-boyfriend. He's been texting me drunk the past few days, whining that he made a mistake in pushing me away. You know the whole ordeal, blah, blah, blah, I want you back, come to Seattle, blah."

Sky's core temperature plummeted, her smile straining at the edges. This was the same ex Mia had been ready to settle down with, and he'd been the one to dump her. All of that formed a recipe for getting back together. Between Mia's mom's imminent move to Austin and now her ex begging for her back, the idea of Mia staying seemed an impossible dream.

"What are you thinking about doing?" Sky asked, even as a brittle casing coated her heart once more. She plucked a few more tortellini from the plate, though they tasted ashen on her tongue.

Mia cast her a sharp glance. "Is this even comfortable for us to be talking about? He's just being a pest, and I didn't want to make you feel awkward."

Sky shrugged. "We're friends, right? Isn't this the sort of stuff friends talk about?"

She hated herself the moment the words came out and Mia's gaze darkened.

If she were being honest, Sky was jealous, plain as

day. Yet, she had no right to be when she alone kept them apart.

Part of her, the part that dreamed and hoped and longed to take daring risks, wanted to buy a ring and propose today—that's how damn sure she felt about Mia Brownstone. However, every time she opened her mouth, memories of the past halted her. All she could think about were the pep talks Jamie used to give her when she talked about her unrequited crush on Mia, the hope gleaming in her sister's eyes.

How fast that all got robbed from her when Jamie died.

If things fell apart with Mia, the other part of her twisted up inside, like she'd be letting her sister down. Sky couldn't bear that.

If things fell apart between them, she'd be losing another person from her younger years—for good.

"Yeah, friends," Mia responded, her voice wooden. She sucked in an unsteady breath and scrolled through her phone. "Derek's offering me all of the things he should've before I ever left Seattle—that he was ready to settle down and didn't realize, and that he misses what we had."

"Do you?" Sky asked, unable to contain the rising panic at those words. She was going to lose Mia. It was only a matter of time. Everyone left.

Memories of her sister paraded around in her mind like a ghost, melding with the lonely months after Mia left. She used to drive past Mia's house only to realize she didn't live there anymore, or stroll down the Riverwalk, waiting to spot her best friend.

Mia shrugged. "What we had in the beginning? Sure. He was sweet, outgoing, and made me laugh. My track record sucks. My own dad left me when I was a kid, and my mother's the ice queen who ditched me for her boyfriends ever since I could fend for myself. I've wanted to be someone's first for so long it's been killing me, to be honest."

Sky chewed on her lip. "Friend, lover, whatever we are—you're always my first, Mia B." Even if she wasn't brave enough to dive in the deep end with Mia, she could at least tell her this truth now.

"Until when, beautiful?" Mia murmured, her voice scraping above a whisper. "What happens when you find a girlfriend you're willing to commit to?"

"There won't be anyone for me," Sky responded, feeling those words in her bones tonight. Mia would go back to Derek or get sick of her indecision, and Sky would be stuck here, too afraid of everyone abandoning her to claim the one woman she wanted.

Mia shook her head. "I don't know how you can stay in limbo. I've always needed to keep moving forward." Slight sadness tinged her words, and Sky wanted to take the pain away, even though she'd been the one to cause it.

Instead, Sky rested a hand on Mia's thigh and squeezed. "Just another reason you're going to spit in your mother's eye and claim what you want."

Mia leaned against Sky, a soft exhalation escaping her in the process. "That's what I'm attempting. I'll clean up in the kitchen, so why don't you set up a board game and we can play tonight?"

"Think if I nab a deck of cards, we can attempt strip poker?" Sky asked, offering a toothy grin.

Mia ran the tip of her tongue over her glossy lower lip and reached her thumb under the strap of her camisole, elevating the gorgeous curve of her tits. "Think you can handle this? I'm a mean poker player, and I'll have you down to nothing after a few hands." Mia paused to scan over the length of Sky's body, and her eyes brightened in response. "Actually, that sounds like a brilliant idea. Strip poker it is."

Sky grinned and headed over to her living room to root out one of her packs of cards. Even though the pressure of their earlier conversation had evaporated with the change of subject, the complicated tangle of her thoughts remained. The buzz of Mia's phone sounded behind her, but she didn't turn around. Mia might be done with Derek, but her words lingered, clanging around over and over again.

Sky knew better than anyone Mia wouldn't stay in this limbo for long.

Once the quarantine lifted, the dynamic woman would be heading toward a future…

Without her.

CHAPTER FOURTEEN

ANOTHER WEEK PASSED, AND DEREK WAS RELENTLESS. He'd started out with the occasional text, but their chats had gotten more regular even though she had no interest in getting back together with him. She'd made that clear from the outset, but she hoped she could salvage some of the friendships she'd lost in the wreckage of their relationship, as if her entire time there hadn't been a waste.

What made things worse was ever since Sky found out Derek had been texting her all the time, the woman pulled away. Just the slightest bit. While most might not notice, few knew Skylar Jenkins as well as she did. Mia wanted to grab her by the shirt sometimes and shake sense into her—their chemistry was next level, and they had the comfortable ease in their communication that would translate perfectly into a relationship. She could see this so clearly, and yet Sky continued to evade her every attempt to push the matter a little further.

Sky was everything she wanted in a partner, and she found it far too easy to lie back and daydream of the future they could claim together.

If only the woman could break past the steel bars she'd encaged herself in.

Tomorrow was the anniversary of Jamie's death, though, and if anything, Sky's walls had fortified from mud bricks to concrete. The queen of self-sabotage was determined to shut her out, though Sky needed someone more than ever right now.

Mia sat up from the project she'd been working on. Her sketchpad lay on her lap, and pencils and ink pens scattered around her while she continued her current piece. She'd lost herself in the headiness of sketching and inking, something she'd forgotten about until this quarantine. The hour had grown late and her back stiffer than ever. On top of that, she needed to pee after the back to back drinks of cider, then water, and then coffee she'd downed.

Sky's door edged open a crack—she'd jumped in on a Zoom chat with Aubrey. Mia straightened up and snuck to the door, preferring to use the good bathroom. Not like the other one was bad, but the one attached to Sky's bedroom was better.

Mia snuck by, trying not to disturb Sky. With her earbuds in, Sky didn't glance back, staring at her friend's face in the glow of the computer screen. Mia slipped into the bathroom with finesse, the door not even creaking as she brought it shut. Mia was about to stride over to the toilet when the fringes of their conversation reached her.

"When this is over, we're doing a Rehoboth trip, you, me, and Kyle." Aubrey's voice came out clear over the speakers. "You bringing anyone with you this year, or are you going solo?"

"Uh." Sky paused, and some rustling sounded.

Mia lived in the pause for far too long, clutching her fist to her chest. Sky had refused to give her a straight answer, but maybe she would for other friends.

"Going solo," Sky said, her voice solemn.

Mia sagged against the door. Tears pricked her eyes. Maybe she'd fucked them up in the first place by never realizing Sky's crush all those years ago, by ditching her best friend when she needed her more than ever. But she'd believed this thing between them would be endgame. That Sky would pull her head out of her ass and realize they'd found a once-in-a-life-time opportunity.

That passing this chance by would break them both.

Tears slipped down her cheeks, hot trails of all the questions, longings, and fears she'd kept pent-up until now. Maybe she didn't know where she needed to be after all. When she returned to Wilmington, she'd been so sure she'd made the right move. However, with Mom moving to Austin, Derek begging her to come back to Seattle, and Sky continuing to push her away, what was she even staying for?

She peeled herself away from the door and made a quick walk over to use the toilet, trying to ignore the stickiness on her cheeks. And she wouldn't be able to find comfort in Sky's arms tonight, not after over-hearing that conversation. The water cascaded over her hands as she washed up—no doubt Sky would know she was here now. Mia didn't know what to say anymore.

Overhearing the conversation scraped like rugburn that wouldn't heal, an abrasion on her heart threat-ening to spread. This time living with Sky had been a microcosm of perfection, but when this quarantine ended, she'd be out on her own again—and she'd have to keep moving forward, whether she wanted to or not.

Mia splashed some water on her face to try and clear the trails of her tears before she turned the faucet off. The peak of the virus had hit, and barely anyone left their homes these days, but with the forward strides made on the medical end of things, it was only a matter of time before the officials lifted this. She strode to the door, but her hand froze on the handle.

She didn't hear any sign of conversation, which must mean the chat had ended. Mia's gut clenched tight. She needed to start putting some distance between them, for her own sanity. At least, after tomorrow.

Mia sucked in a steadying breath and turned the knob, stepping out into the bedroom. Sky sat on the unmade bed, looking gorgeous and rumpled like the blankets around her. She glanced at Mia and patted the bed.

"I didn't hear you come in. Want to head to bed early?" Something seductive and sweet lingered in Sky's tone, but Mia couldn't take that right now.

Right now, she wanted to run out the door of this apartment and find her own space to hide. But with shelter-in-place being enforced, there was nowhere else she could go. Heat welled in her eyes again. She wouldn't be able to fake anything tonight.

She also knew Sky still wouldn't give her answers.

Mia ran her fingers through her hair. "Nah, I think I'm going to stretch out on the futon tonight." The words came out fainter than intended as she took careful steps toward the door.

Sky sat up straight on the bed, her brows drawing tight together in concern. "Everything okay, Mia B? Did I do something wrong?"

Mia shook her head, brushing her fingertips across her forehead. "Just a migraine. I figure I'll sleep it off."

"If you want to lay by me, I'll stroke your head," Sky offered. "Maybe that'll help?"

Mia's lips pressed into a thin line. The woman was drowning and resuscitating her at the same time with this sweetness. Not like this back and forth pull would matter for long. Their arrangement would all be over once she moved out. "Sounds tempting, but I'm bad company tonight," she murmured before stepping through the door and bringing it shut behind her.

She tiptoed over to the futon and grabbed one of the blankets folded in a stack beside it, unused apart from curling up together on the balcony or snuggling on the couches while watching a movie. This place held landmines all over, and every step forward brought a fresh wave of pain.

Mia barely reached the futon by the time the tears started coursing down her cheeks again. She wrapped the blanket around herself and curled up on the futon, facing the wall. Her mouth remained closed, her tears silent, but her shoulders shook with the weight of her frustrations. She'd been fragile glass and the comment had been the steel bat swing she'd needed to shatter.

She had to separate herself from this arrangement before she got any more attached. Just because Sky had been one of her best friends didn't mean the woman would be willing to commit to the forever type of relationship Mia searched for. She hated the way her chest squeezed like a tightening fist, how she'd read into those lingering looks in Sky's eyes and hoped for more.

Every time Mia fell for someone, she dove right off the cliff's edge, and every time she splintered to pieces, she lost another fragment of herself.

Times like this, it grew all too easy to see how her mother's bitterness had formed and solidified, gluing the pieces into place over time until they became a seamless part of her. Mia couldn't let that happen. She couldn't become that person.

Which meant once the quarantine ended, she

would have to put some distance between her and Sky before she moved on.

Mia closed her eyes, though her heart's aching pulse kept her awake far longer than she'd anticipated. Eventually, her breaths evened, and she drifted to sleep.

———

THE NEXT MORNING, MIA WOKE UP TO BRIGHT LIGHT streaming through the windows, a gorgeous day when it had no right to be. Despite the way she'd fallen asleep last night, as she set the coffee to brewing and leaned against the kitchen counter, one event dominated her mind.

Seven years had passed since she'd let the brunt of Jamie's death slam into her like this. The first anniversary had been the hardest, but when she'd headed across the country, somehow being removed from Sky, her family, and the locations back home softened the blow. She didn't forget, per se, but she'd distracted herself.

She had the luxury to. Jamie's death had left a deep score mark that could never be sandpapered out, but what she'd experienced was nothing compared to Sky.

Sky's world had changed overnight, and she'd

watched her best friend lose hope for a future, like colors drained off a canvas. By the time Mia had left for college, that hadn't shifted, and Sky clung to those altered beliefs like the memories of her sister. The coffee finished brewing, spitting the last dark drops into the carafe, and Mia grabbed two mugs. Today, she could put her own feelings aside, because today more than ever, Sky needed her best friend.

The door to Sky's bedroom creaked, and a pang of regret throbbed through Mia at not being in bed with the woman when she woke up. She never slept as good as she did by Sky's side, their limbs tangled together while they held onto each other for dear life.

Sky didn't meet her eyes, trudging over to the kitchen as she slid her fingers through her shorter strands. She'd tossed on a gray sweatshirt and black basketball shorts, walking her way barefoot. Dark circles under her eyes made it clear she'd barely slept.

"I got the coffee going," Mia offered, pouring the steaming liquid into the two mugs. Before Sky stepped into the kitchen, she'd already fixed their cups up the normal way they took them. Mia pushed the one mug over to Sky, who slumped against the counter.

"Thanks, babe," Sky said, her voice coming out soft and tentative, as if it hadn't been used in ages.

Quiet lapsed through the kitchen as they both

leaned against the counter sipping at their piping hot coffees. Mia wanted to reach out and offer comfort, but she didn't know what to do or say in this situation. With the way Sky stiffened at every mention of her sister, she clearly hadn't come close to healing from the gaping loss yet, and Mia didn't want to push her into uncomfortable territory.

"Did you know mortality and mortal come from the Latin word mors, which means death?" Sky commented as she sipped her coffee.

"I'm guessing you have an entire arsenal of morbid facts for today," Mia commented, sliding in closer to Sky so their legs touched.

Sky glanced at her and offered a half-smile. "Yeah, though, usually my folks are the ones privy to them. We'd always go down to the cemetery and pay her a visit." Sky sucked in a breath only to exhale as if she released a part of her soul. "Except with all of the restrictions due to TELA, Jamie's cemetery is closed. And we can't even meet up together because of the lockdowns."

Mia's heart hurt. Even more lives were being lost from this virus, and so many couldn't mourn their loved ones together. She hated that Sky and her family would be apart today.

"Well, fuck, that's shitty," Mia murmured, leaning

in more against Sky. She could feel the woman's pain in the static tension of the air, and God, she wanted to take it away so badly. No matter what happened between her and Sky, she'd fight to preserve their friendship this time. "What can we do?"

Sky's eyes widened, her brows going up in surprise, as if she didn't realize Mia would be with her in this. "I'm going to Facetime with my folks later, but you're welcome to join me."

Mia eyed the booze hutch in the living room. "Why don't we have some drinks tonight. If you want to stay quiet, we can do that, but if you want to talk about Jamie, we can do that too. Whatever you need."

Sky leaned against Mia, her arms wrapping around to pull her tight. "You're a goddamn miracle, you know that? I've been freaking out about this day for the past week, but having you here with me… it makes a difference."

Mia swallowed hard, sinking against Sky. The woman's scent surrounded her, all cedar and spice, and her eyes prickled with unshed tears at how much she'd come to treasure the feel of Sky by her side. How attached she'd grown to the connection between them.

She didn't want to let it go.

CHAPTER FIFTEEN

After going online to talk to her parents with Mia by her side, Sky still hadn't cried.

She'd brimmed on the verge of tears all day, the aching feeling that dwelled beneath the skin waiting to burst free, but the whole quarantine made the anniversary feel a bit surreal. Not standing in front of her sister's resting place but instead relaxing in her apartment like this was any other day felt wrong.

Sky curled up on the couch, clutching tight to the bottle of Jack she'd pulled from her hutch. Except today would never just be any day.

She didn't know how to explain back then, and she sure as hell couldn't now, but something fundamental inside of her had cracked the evening the cops came to their door instead of Jamie. She'd been searching for years to find a way to patch over the emptiness, a hollow ache that sometimes rose in her chest, a grief too terrible to face, and yet she'd never found a solution.

All she'd learned was she'd become far too broken to embrace the kind of love that meant forever, because that evening, she had learned forever didn't exist.

She took a swig of Jack, letting the whiskey wash down her throat, burning through all of the emptiness.

Mia took a seat beside her on the futon, curling into her side. "What do you normally say around the grave?" she asked, her voice gentle.

Today, Mia entered the room with a quieter air around her, like the sky on a gray autumn day. Sky could feel Mia's focus on her as her best friend guided their steps.

"Mom cries while Dad and I stand stoic," Sky murmured, clutching tighter to the neck of the bottle. "There's not a lot of talk, just a lot of static silences."

Mia pursed her lips. "Do you mind if I say something?" she asked. "I know Jamie's grave isn't here, but… there are a few things I wanted to tell her."

Sky's heart tore in two, somehow existing outside of her chest today. She offered a nod and passed the bottle over to Mia in case the woman needed liquid courage. Not like she would. She was the bravest person Sky had ever met with the way she faced her feelings and kept fighting.

Mia clutched the bottle of whiskey tight, but she didn't take a drink. Instead, she leaned in closer to Sky, their shoulders and thighs bumping against each other.

"Jamie, I fucked up. I should've been back here to talk with you ages ago," Mia started, her voice shaky. While Mia stared at the opposite wall, Sky didn't have to stretch to imagine standing in the cemetery at Jamie's grave. She could smell the fresh dirt and feel the coolness from the surrounding tombstones like she did every year.

Sky's breath rattled from her at the outburst of emotion heavy in the room. She reached over and slid her fingers through Mia's, clutching her hand tight.

"Right now, I'm in this transition point where sometimes I don't even know who the hell I am," Mia continued. "But that's just making me remember you more right now. You knew yourself and always seemed so sure of yourself, even in high school, which was hell for most folks. I can't help but wonder what you might've been like in college. Probably going for your master's degree, ready to head into law like you wanted to and absolutely crushing it."

Sky clutched her hand even tighter, her nails digging into Mia's palm. The tears burned in her eyes even as she fought them.

How many times had she wondered what Jamie might be doing right now?

Her little sister had shone supernova, so when the light flickered out, Sky was left fumbling in the dark.

The scent of pork roast still made her stomach turn—she remembered heaving it all up that night.

Sky still crumbled to her knees every time she heard "Janie's Got a Gun" by Aerosmith because all she could hear was Jamie changing the name to hers.

She still couldn't read *Pride and Prejudice*, because the classic had been Jamie's favorite, and she couldn't get past the first words without the tears flowing.

"Anyway, I just wanted to tell you that I miss you, Jamie Jenkins," Mia continued, her voice thick. "I miss your eager laugh and the glint in your eyes you'd get when you bothered your sister. I miss the blunt way you'd tell the truth of a situation. The world might be moving forward, but we haven't forgotten you."

The heat intensified around Sky's eyes, and the first hot tears coursed down her cheeks. She hadn't needed to say anything—Mia captured her feelings perfectly. Mia lapsed into silence, and they both leaned against each other, the connection of their bodies the sole thing she held onto right now.

Jamie had been leaving a friend's house, crossing the street.

The driver had been drunk.

She'd never stood a chance once the car slammed into her.

So fast, Sky's life altered. So fast, people started expecting her to speak in the past tense, even though her sister had just. Been. There.

She'd picked up her phone far too many times to call Jamie only to realize there wouldn't be a response on the other line. She still hadn't deleted her name from her address book—she didn't know if she ever could. The tears ran unchecked, Sky's shoulders trembling in response. Mia nestled in deeper, her eyes glossy.

Sky hadn't let herself cry in years, afraid of how she'd crack. But watching Mia speak the words trapped inside her for too long coaxed the tears out until they ran freely.

"God, I miss her," Sky murmured, her words barely audible. She couldn't stop the tears streaming down her cheeks if she tried, as if her walls cracked and all of that grief she'd pinned back escaped.

"Me too, beautiful," Mia responded, stroking her fingers through her hair. "Me too."

The bottle of Jack lay forgotten on the ground beside them. Sky leaned against Mia's chest, letting those tears flow, and Mia clutched her back like she might somehow disappear too. Hours, minutes, seconds passed in a silence swallowed by the consuming grief that hung heavy in the air. Still, Sky clung to Mia, as if she might get to keep one thing in her life from her past.

<hr>

THE HOUR TURNED LATE FAR TOO FAST, AND THE gentle night breezes swept in through her open windows. Her tears had dried long before, and she and Mia ate heated leftovers for dinner, grabbing a necessary cup of hot tea to go along with them. No matter how the liquid warmed her up for a moment, nothing filled the hollowness that remained. Sky leaned against the couch, clutching the porcelain between her palms.

Sky glanced to where Mia sat at the breakfast nook, sipping at the remnants of her black tea. Strands of Mia's hair tumbled down to her shoulders, the chestnut waves she'd run her fingers through a thousand times. Her ocean eyes weighted with the same weariness, yet the woman had never looked more beautiful.

Even if she couldn't say the words out loud, they emerged every time Sky glanced at Mia.

I love you.

Mia was brave, resilient, and strong in ways she longed to be, and the more time she spent around her, the more she began to heal.

Truth be told, the change terrified and enraptured her at the same time.

Mia wandered over to slump next to Sky, their shoulders brushing against each other. Desire rose inside her, this desperate, trembling need to feel—something—anything beyond this numbness on the anniversary of Jamie's death.

"Hey," Sky murmured, drawing Mia's gaze to meet hers. "Stay with me tonight?" Her tongue dried at asking for anything from this woman. She had no right, not after the wedge she'd been pushing between them. But based on Mia's look, Sky might not be the only one who needed to feel whole tonight.

Mia nodded and offered her hand. Sky rested her palm in Mia's as the woman rose from the couch, bringing Sky with her. Together, they took careful steps toward the bedroom, as if at any moment, the tenuous connection between them might shatter, as if one of them might pull away. Still, her heart lurched, following Mia to something that wasn't a lust-fueled frenzy. This was everything her heart tried to deny, baring herself to this woman in a way she couldn't retract.

They entered her dim bedroom, the scent of pine incense heavy in the air from when she'd burnt it earlier, trying to even her breaths. She followed as Mia led her over to the rumpled, unmade bed and slid onto the mattress. Sky's heartbeat quickened at the sight of the beautiful woman who had stolen her heart long ago, covered in paint stains and sarcasm. She settled into bed next to her and slipped her fingers along the side of Mia's neck until they wove through her hair as she cupped the back of the woman's head.

Sky leaned in, pressing her lips to Mia's. She tasted like black tea and warmth, like sunlight. The emptiness in Sky's chest ached even more ferociously, as if she might never capture this again, as if this euphoria would continue to slip out of her grasp, over and over. She claimed Mia's mouth, sweeping her tongue in to possess this woman, if only for tonight.

Mia's fingers slipped beneath the hem of her shirt, tugging it up. Sky broke the kiss, breathless as she pulled her sweatshirt over her head and tossed it off the side of the bed. She returned to Mia's lips, settling her palm on the curve of her gorgeous hip. Her mouth traveled down the column of Mia's neck. The woman's skin was so soft Sky couldn't get enough of her. A throaty noise came from Mia, one that sent a pulse down her spine, all the way to her core.

As her nipples brushed against the flimsy fabric of Mia's shirt, they pebbled, and the throb between her legs grew with each fevered kiss. Sky slipped her hand to the waistband of Mia's pants, hooking her thumb into the elastic of her panties. For a breath, she separated from Mia just to look her in the eyes. Sky chewed her lower lip as she stared into that passion-drenched gaze. Mia made her feel again when the numbness threatened to devour her whole.

Mia shimmied her hips, helping as Sky drew the pants down her legs to toss them into the pile.

"I think we did this a little backward," Mia murmured, a slight grin playing on her swollen lips.

Sky shook her head and brought her fingers to cup Mia's pussy, juices brimming from the folds. God, she was fucking sexy. Mia's breath hitched in her throat as Sky glided her fingertips up the crease before curling them around the hem of Mia's shirt. A moment later, that hit the floor as well, leaving this stunning woman bare before her.

Mia's waves splayed out on her white bedsheets, and Sky drank in the details from the freckle on Mia's left breast to the tempting curve of her hips. The light glossed over her lush lips. She could spend a lifetime with this woman and never tire of learning and exploring every last facet. Sky didn't want to stop licking and sucking every inch of her body, but she longed to see Mia unravel before her. She needed to.

Sky reached down, slipping her fingers between the soaked folds of Mia's pussy as she continued to bite and suck along her collarbone, her traps, licking the tip of her nipple just to watch her shiver. Sky began to stroke at Mia's clit until those shallow breaths turned into a melody of their own. Mia's scent surrounded her, all peaches and summer, like they'd been vaulted to a different time of lazy warm days and endless sky.

Sky's chest ached as Mia moaned in her ear. She leaned down, licking and sucking at the woman's pebbled nipples, enjoying how Mia's hips bucked up every time. Sky placed kisses between Mia's breasts, her collarbone, until she reached the sensitive pulse that fluttered on her neck and planted a featherlight kiss there. She slipped two fingers inside Mia, and the woman's breath hitched.

"You feel so damn perfect," Sky murmured as she pumped her fingers inside Mia.

Mia's lashes fluttered open, and their eyes met. Her mouth opened as if words rested on the tip of her tongue, but they never escaped her lips. Sky could see the tenderness in her gaze, soft yearning, like watercolors or handwritten letters. Sky pumped faster, strands of her hair drifting past her forehead. Sweat prickled on her skin as the sight of Mia flushed beneath her got her hotter than ever. They'd fucked every way imaginable ever since the first night, yet this felt different.

The desire grew heady in the air between them still, but this connection was every phrase she'd underlined by fingertip in her favorite books, every passage she'd reread because it made her heart ache, because those words made her feel the faint flutter of hope despite the world's attempt to deaden her.

She continued to pump her fingers inside Mia, loving the way the woman's hips thrust up toward her, how her wanton moans lit the air in response. She couldn't help but swallow them up, leaning down to capture her lips. The ache in her core grew unbearable with how turned on she'd become. Their breasts crushed together, her sensitized nipples brushing against Mia's velvet skin. Sky drifted her thumb over

Mia's clit as she thrust in, the woman's moans growing louder and louder.

Mia gripped her shoulders, her nails digging into the skin as sweat beaded across her forehead, an exquisite flush across her cheeks, her chest. A cry rang out as Mia's thighs clamped around her. The pulse around Sky's fingers didn't stop her as she continued to pump inside Mia until she collapsed onto the sheets beneath her. Sky slowly pulled her fingers out, giving them a lick. Mia looked at her, a feverish desire in her eyes.

"Your turn, beautiful," Mia murmured, crooking her fingers. "Shorts off."

Sky chewed on her lip as she pushed up and tossed her pants and underwear over the side of the bed with the rest of the pile. She climbed back toward Mia, who had turned to her side. They faced each other, both stark naked and lying on the bed. All of Sky's previous confidence vanished as she was left a melting mess before this woman she'd been smitten with for half of her life.

"Come here," Mia said, her voice gentle. She guided Sky's shaking thigh over the top of hers and slipped deft fingers to the soaked folds between her legs. Mia leaned forward, beginning to kiss Sky, all languid strokes, soft puffs of breath, and the heat of their bodies melding together.

Sky closed her eyes, surrendering to the sensation of Mia pressed against her, fucking her into oblivion. The current of pleasure threatened to carry her away, and after the day she had, she flowed along with it, just letting go. All of the pain and the fears melted off her in this moment alone, surrounded by Mia's sweet scent, the tang of her swollen lips, and the seductive sensations of the way she thrust her fingers inside her.

Sky had been brimming from the moment they began, so it didn't take long before she spilled over the edge. Strands of Mia's silken hair brushed against her arm, their breasts pressed flush together, and Mia thrust deep, holding her fingers there as Sky came. Her back arched with the intensity of the orgasm, how it pulsed through her like some cleansing force that allowed her reprieve, if only for a moment.

She came back to the cool mattress beneath her, the rumpled sheets tangled around them, and Mia's beautiful eyes, navy in this light, staring at her. Sky sucked in a shaky breath. Mia pulled her fingers out and rested her hand on Sky's hip, not budging from where they lay.

They both remained there in the silence, unable to

look away as their breaths steadied. Mia's leg slipped over hers, and Sky slung her arm over Mia's waist, but neither bothered to move. The dim lamp barely cast enough light in this room, the amber rays coating every surface. Sky memorized the pulse of Mia's throat as she breathed, the freckles across her cheeks, and the slight frown to her mouth when she grew somber.

Something as immense as a thunderstorm spread between them, leaving her silent in the wake. And still, those words fluttered with every breath, every thump of her heart.

I love you.

She opened her mouth as if she'd ever be bold enough to speak them, but when she glanced back at Mia, the woman's eyes were closed, and her breaths came out in the even rhythm of slumber.

Sky held on tighter, sinking into the sensation of this precious woman in her arms as her eyes closed and her world grayed around the edges.

CHAPTER SIXTEEN

THE REST OF THE WEEK PASSED, AND NEITHER MIA NOR Sky spoke of that night. They hadn't tried to have sex since, and Mia couldn't decide how she felt about their impasse. Even though her feelings couldn't be extinguished, sinking deeper into the fantasy of a relationship with Sky wouldn't help either of them. However, the other part of her longed to claim any last moment they might have together like this before the quarantine lifted.

And then, Monday morning bright and early, the email arrived in Mia's inbox.

Her new house was available for her to move in.

She spent most of her workday trying to wrangle how to tell Sky, because truth be told, she didn't want to leave. The constant touch and the loving gazes she got from the woman could keep her tethered for the rest of her life, but Sky would never take the step to admit what she wanted. Besides, Mia couldn't afford to keep her stuff at the storage unit any longer.

Mia exited the side room that had become her office and stepped into the scent of sizzling beef wafting through the air. Sky stood in the kitchen, flipping burgers on the stovetop. The woman always looked natural there—she moved with a familiar grace from working as a chef.

"Hope you like burgers," Sky called over once she caught sight of Mia. "They'll be done in a minute."

"Love 'em. Let me get the plates," Mia said, falling into their same old routine. The idea of heading to an empty house away from this comfort caused her chest to ache. But she didn't have a future waiting for her here. Sky never promised her forever.

As always, Sky went overboard on the food front with all of her embellishments. She'd baked home-made fries with rosemary that smelled fantastic, and arranged a bowl of fresh salad filled with spring mix, sliced cucumbers, and radishes to go along with every-thing. Mia carried the bowl with the tongs over to the breakfast nook and then passed the plates over to Sky, who popped the burgers onto toasted buns, squeezed the condiments on, and dressed them with thinly sliced tomatoes, onions, and a handful of lettuce. Sky glanced up and their eyes met, the soft look in Sky's socking her in the chest.

Any minute now, she would splinter apart, and her heart tangled like brambles.

"These look fucking fantastic," Mia murmured, carrying the plates over to the breakfast nook. No matter how delicious they smelled, her stomach churned enough that they'd taste like chalk right now.

They both sat, and Sky began to wolf down her burger. A wistful tug in her chest occurred every time she glanced Sky's way. The woman possessed this earthy sort of beauty that entranced her every time, a solidness she wanted to sink into.

The urge to rip the day-old Band-Aid off grew stronger than ever, and before she could help herself, she blurted, "I got an email from my landlord today," knowing she couldn't backtrack from this one.

Sky looked up, freezing mid-bite of the burger.

Mia tugged on the end of her hair, hating how abrupt her words came out. No other way about it though—neither of them wanted to face this news. "They want me to move in tomorrow. I'll slowly begin bringing stuff from my storage unit to the new place over the course of the week. I… already arranged with work to take tomorrow off and get situated."

"Right," Sky said, her voice strained even as she kept a neutral expression. "Well, good for you, Mia B. It's about time you get settled into the city all proper-like."

Even though she could see Sky struggling plain as day, the cavalier comments stung. This was why she couldn't keep doing this. She'd fallen in love with her best friend who might not ever be able to commit.

Sky stared at her sandwiches. "Did you know, during World War I, hamburgers were referred to as liberty sandwiches?"

Mia let out a strangled laugh. She should've known Sky would revert to avoidance, but part of her had wished for something different. Part of her wished Sky would ask her to stay, would tell her this all meant as much to her as it did for Mia. "Yeah, but I bet folks weren't dining on high-end burgers like these ones," Mia said, forcing herself to take a bite.

She chewed, but she could barely taste the rich flavors from the burger.

Tomorrow, she would leave.

WHAT MIA FOUND MIND-BOGGLING WAS HOW SIMPLE packing had been the night before. She'd believed the task would be long and strenuous, but she'd been using all of Sky's things for the entire stay and mostly just needed to pack and fold clothing back into her suitcase. The landlord was leaving the keys in the mailbox at nine in the morning where she'd pick them up and start getting situated—the best they could manage while the quarantine restrictions remained in place.

Last night after Sky had fallen asleep, Mia had brought her suitcase out to the car, sleeping in the clothes she'd wear to the new place. Mia had stopped by Sky's room, the door left open a crack, and she couldn't help but peer in.

The woman looked so peaceful when she slept— the worry crease that sometimes appeared seemed to relax. Her long lashes stood out against the white of her bedding, and her olive skin gleamed in the dim amber lighting.

Mia headed over to the coffeemaker, getting the brew going the way she and Sky always switched off on the task of making the morning coffee. Any minute, the woman would be up, and she'd have to say her goodbye.

It wasn't forever.

It wasn't.

They were still friends, best friends. But this closeness she'd discovered, the soft way Sky moaned, how she curled around Mia in a protective cocoon when they slept together, how she was the first person Mia wanted to see in the morning and the last she wanted to see at night—Mia had fallen hard.

She slipped her purse over her shoulder and nursed a cup of coffee, waiting for Sky to trudge out of her room. The scorching hot liquid bolstered her, giving her bravery she hadn't possessed before.

The door creaked open a minute later, and Sky stumbled out. Her hair was mussed from sleep, and she only wore a sleep shirt with underwear, looking fucking sexier than ever.

"You made coffee?" Sky said, trudging in toward her. "Thanks, babe." Sky looked up, and her gaze settled on the purse slung over Mia's shoulder and held there.

"The owners want me to grab the key bright and early," Mia said, her voice coming out tentative.

Sky let out a grunt and a nod as she rooted around her cupboard for a mug. A desperation rose in Mia's chest, one that grew as frantic as a fish flopping on dry ground.

When Sky turned around, Mia closed the distance between them. She pressed her lips to Sky's, resting her arms on her shoulders. Sky kissed back with the same ferocity, as if agony flooded through her veins too. As if they both knew this could be goodbye. Sky's palms settled around her waist, and Mia devoured the woman's mouth, capturing her lips again and again and again. She sank into the relief of the kiss, the comfort, the sanctuary she'd found here in her best friend's arms.

God, she loved Sky so damn much.

Mia pulled away at last, her heart thundering in her ears. She stared into Sky's eyes. Even if it hurt, she'd regret not speaking up—she always did. She kept her hands resting on Sky's shoulders, the connection offering her the ground to stand upon.

"Look, I know this whole thing was supposed to be no-strings, us dealing with the stressful situation of the quarantine. I also know you've been avoiding this talk from the beginning, and I've given you the pass because I figured you needed it. But I can't keep this pent-up any longer."

Sky's shoulders stiffened beneath her palms, but Mia looked Sky square in the eyes and continued anyway.

"I've always cared about you, Sky, from the moment we became friends. However, when romantic feelings came into the equation, I couldn't help but fall for you. You know I'm in relationships for the long haul, for the idea of sharing a future together, and I know we haven't had 'the talk,' but I can't leave here without knowing what this thing between us is. Because if you say you want a relationship too, I'm yours, no question. I've never found someone I could spend forever with until getting holed away in your tiny apartment during this quarantine. I would love to spend forever with you, Skylar Jenkins."

Mia's heart leapt into her throat, the unsaid sticking there. *But I need you to say it too.*

She'd spilled every hidden thing inside her save one, and Mia stood there, palms resting on Sky's shoulders.

Part of her imagined this fantasy of Sky confessing everything, of them kissing and kissing until clothes came off and she called her landlord to cancel because she'd be living here with the best friend and love of her life.

However, as Sky stared back wide-eyed, her silence told a different tale.

Even if Sky felt the same, even if she cared, she still couldn't offer what Mia needed.

Which meant the time for goodbye had arrived.

The weight in her chest crushed her, stealing the air from her lungs. Yet she somehow managed to extricate herself from Sky's embrace and step back.

Mia tried to ignore the heat pricking her eyes, tears that threatened to fall.

She'd bared everything, but this silent rejection hurt more than she could've anticipated.

"Right, message received. Fuck it," Mia said, thrusting her jaw forward in an attempt to stay strong. "Well, thanks for everything, Sky."

She couldn't manage anything more as she made her way to the door one step at a time. With every drag of her heel, she hoped and prayed for Sky to cry out, to stop her from leaving, to confess everything she saw percolating to the surface in those honey-dark eyes.

Except every step brought more silence, until she reached for the knob and walked out the door.

CHAPTER SEVENTEEN

Three weeks.

Three weeks had passed since Mia moved out, and while they still talked, Sky had fucked up their friendship beyond repair. The worst thing about it all? If she hadn't been so stunned by Mia's confession, she would have done anything to keep Mia in her apartment, in her bed. The words that had glued like epoxy to the roof of her mouth might've unstuck themselves at last. Her place never felt this empty before, but reminders of Mia's presence lingered everywhere.

Including the sketch Mia had left behind of Sky, Jamie, and her back in high school. It may have accumulated a few tearstains after Sky found the piece resting on her countertop after Mia departed.

Sky settled into the booth at Renegades, grateful to be out of the house and back to work. Some restrictions and lighter hours remained in place, but the distraction was the only thing keeping her afloat right now. She'd called Aubs out because she needed someone to shake some sense into her. Chatter flowed around her, the bars and restaurants were creeping back into business in the wake of the TELA virus.

There had been so much panic, so much fear, and yet she'd been encased in this blissful cocoon of sex and love with the woman of her dreams. How she'd let that slip out of her fingers was a goddamn travesty.

Aubs sauntered to the booth, her hair pulled into a ponytail and wearing sleek athletic clothes that highlighted how in shape she remained even after all the time cloistered away. Along the way, she cast a few winks and blew a few kisses to some of the ladies by the bar.

"God, I could fuck my way through this place and still not be satisfied after two months of being caged away from human contact," Aubrey said as she flounced into the seat opposite her. "How are you not on the prowl with all this eye candy here?"

Sky pinched her nape. "I didn't have any problems during the quarantine."

Aubrey turned to face her, full attention swinging her way like a baseball bat. "No fucking way. You and that complete fox you've been obsessed with forever hooked up? Why the hell are you out here with me and not holed away fucking the daylights out of each other?"

"About that," Sky said, scratching the back of her hand and refusing to look at Aubs. Her whiskey sour sat untouched beside her, and she'd ordered Aubrey a coffee porter, which she'd tipped back. "I fucked up. She told me how she felt and everything—that she was in this for keeps if I was, how she wanted to be my girlfriend, and I... couldn't respond."

Aubrey paused and placed her beer down with a clink on the countertop. "Skylar Christine Jenkins," she said in her most imperious tone.

"My middle name is Meredith," Sky muttered, running her fingers through her hair. A lecture would come, and Aubrey was the one who'd give it to her. She needed the tongue lashing, bad, which was why she'd called Aubs in the first place.

"Sky," Aubs said, her voice quieter.

Sky snapped her head up in surprise to look at Aubrey—that hadn't been the righteous indignation she'd expected.

"I've watched you keep every girl you dated at a distance for years. I'm not surprised the one who's important, the one who already knows you—all of you —is the one you were going to push away. You've been grieving for a long time now, but did you ever really deal with it?"

Sky's mouth dried. The school counselor sessions back then had been useless forced-positivity drivel that just made Sky angry. Her parents never wanted to talk about Jamie's death, and neither had she.

Aubs leaned in, drawing her attention. "Look. I've got a great therapist I've been seeing for a while, and if you want, I can give you her info." Aubrey never talked like this—they skated on the superficial.

Sky ran a hand through her hair. She'd considered therapy for years, but every time, the thought numbed her. The therapist would leave her feeling hollower, resurrecting her past. Except, when Mia spoke about Jamie on the anniversary—even though she'd cried, for once, the empty ache in her chest had eased.

If it meant maybe fixing some of the mess she'd made between her and Mia, she wanted to try.

"Yeah, I'd like that," Sky said, her voice coming out hoarse. She took a sip of her whiskey sour, relishing the sweetness. The scent of rich beer, fragrant perfumes, and dark, treated wood wafted through the air, but she missed the scent of peaches more than ever.

"Good," Aubs responded, slapping her palms on the table. "That aside, I'm invoking the Rehoboth Pact."

Sky wrinkled her nose. This was what she knew would be coming.

Five years ago, when she, Aubrey, and Kyle began going on their yearly trip to Rehoboth, they made a deal with each other. All had stacked up a fair number of failed relationships, each shouldering their own damage, but if one of them ever found "the one" and tried to push her away, then the others would step in.

The Rehoboth Pact, a yearly talked about but never utilized deal... until now.

"Hey, I'm just excited to be able to invoke it—first time ever," Aubs said, digging her elbows into the splintered surface of the bar. Hollers and shouts sounded all around them, everyone enjoying the group gatherings after so long spent away. None of their celebrations distracted her—Sky's focus remained on Aubrey.

"After five seconds around the two of you, I could see Mia was your 'one.' And if you already know she feels the same way, then if you don't go after her now, you're going to carry this regret with you for the rest of your life," Aubs said, her tone holding an iron edge. The woman could be scary as shit when she wanted to be. "Look, Sky. If I had the sort of connection you and Mia do, would I be hitting up someone new every time I come here? Hell no. Not everyone has the chance, and if you don't take it, I'm going to break the chick code and swoop in to romance her myself."

Even though Aubrey never would, the words ignited a fire inside her. The idea of Mia in someone else's arms, falling asleep in someone else's bed, sitting and sketching on quiet nights next to someone else, hell, she'd die.

"Don't you dare," Sky responded, even though there wasn't any heat in her voice.

Aubs arched a brow. "What are you going to do about it?"

"I know what to do." Sky heaved a sigh. She didn't even need to question the next step, because she understood Mia Brownstone better than anyone else on the planet. She just hoped she hadn't lost her chance.

"You know I'm following up with you, right?" Aubs commented, her brow still arched. "If a week passes and you haven't gotten up off your ass to tell her how you feel, tick, tick, tick, doll. I'll call her and get her into my bed that night."

Sky lifted her middle finger, even though she caught the hint of a grin playing on Aubrey's lips. The woman would do what was needed to provoke her, but at the end of the day, Aubrey always had loyalty on speed dial. Sky could trust her.

Just like she should've trusted Mia.

She sucked back the rest of her whiskey sour, the liquid burning the rest of the way. The glass's thunk echoed as she slammed it onto the hardwood tabletop. "I think I'll at least need another two or three before I work up the nerve to send the text."

"I'll grab the drinks tonight," Aubrey said, "as long as you wingman for me later. Unlike you, who's been getting some, I've been starving. And you tell anyone else I see a therapist and I'll slit your throat. It'll ruin my brand image of crazy, unstable, and loving it."

Sky crossed her heart over her chest. "Secret's safe with me."

Aubs hopped up and sauntered over to the bar to order more drinks. Sky leaned back in her seat and stared at the ceiling. Her chest wound tighter than ever, but she'd find a way to get the words out, even if the idea shocked her system like a springtime blizzard.

Aubrey wasn't wrong—she regretted letting Mia leave that day without saying something—anything back.

Even if Mia turned her down and fractured her heart, or even more terrifying—if she wanted her, broken pieces and all—she had stayed silent for too long.

Sky couldn't keep living in this limbo any longer.

CHAPTER EIGHTEEN

"Make sure to keep the winter clothes in separate boxes from the summer ones," Mia's mother called out from the hallway.

Mia had agreed to help her mother pack before she moved at the end of the week, mostly because she wanted to do her part to see her only family before they relocated to Austin. Truth be told, the way her mom decided to up and leave still stung after how much guilt she'd given Mia when she moved away to Seattle. And of course, after five minutes of trying to pack with her control-freak mother, she was about to tear her hair out.

"Crazy, I thought all those down jackets were supposed to go in summer attire," Mia drawled, unable to help her sarcasm in return.

Her mother poked in through the door. "Very funny, Mia." Her hair was pulled into a loose bun, and she appeared more dressed down than normal in stained jeans and a wrinkled gray shirt. "How's your new place?"

Mia shrugged. Honestly, the new house was beautiful. There was plenty of space, a green lawn out back, and some gorgeous cherry and Dogwood trees in full bloom. However, her bed had become achingly cold at night, and sometimes the quiet grew deafening.

She missed Sky's apartment, but even more so, she missed Sky.

Mia missed cuddling on the futon to watch a random paranormal show on Netflix together, sitting down to share dinner with her, and making jokes about the day. She missed how Sky nuzzled against her and found any excuse to touch her in ways that made her feel so damn whole she'd burst. There wasn't a break-up, per se, because they'd never been seeing each other, but even her split with Derek hadn't haunted her like this.

"That bad?" Mom asked as she bustled behind her, snagging a few of the paisley dresses laid out on the bed to start folding them up. "You can always come move to Austin if you're not finding any good spots around here."

Like she wanted to uproot again. Mia was just trying to find a place she belonged, and Mom's snap decision hadn't helped. Still, she couldn't say she'd miss having her mother in close proximity. The distance in Seattle had been a blessing to their relationship, keeping them from clawing each other's eyes out.

Mia shook her head. "No, the place itself is nice. Just going through a bit of a spell over someone."

Not like she wanted to broach the subject with her mother. The ice queen wasn't the sort of woman who'd be warm and fuzzy about her coming out as bisexual, and Mom only liked discussing her relationships when they were falling apart.

"Still harping over Derek?" Mom asked, pushing past her to grab the summer box she'd been working on.

Mia rolled her eyes and stepped to the opposite side of the bed. Why she'd even come to help was a mystery when her mother would correct everything she did. She grabbed one of the ugly A-line dresses on the bed and began to fold it up.

"No, Mom," Mia said between gritted teeth. Times like this, she missed having Sky around who knew just from a single look that she had a disagreement with her mother. No one else bothered to understand her the same way.

"How could you have met someone else?" Mom asked, pushing regardless. Little passion existed behind her voice, just a solid, cement persistence. "We were under quarantine the past two months. Don't tell me you found yourself all moony-eyed over an online relationship. Dear, those never work out."

Mia's chest grew hot, the way it always did when her mother took a spade and plunged the tip right through her heart. "Because Sky and I were together, Mom," she spat out. "I'm bisexual."

Well, that hadn't been how she wanted to come out to her mother. A moment later, mortification settled across her skin like melting ice cream.

Silence spread through the room, leaving the scent of mothballs and a whole lot of awkwardness.

"When did you learn this about yourself?" Mom asked, her voice stiff.

"In college," Mia said, resigning herself to another fight with her mother. "I had a girlfriend for a little while before I met Derek."

Her mother let out a little "Hmm," and then busied herself with folding up another dress to put into the summer box. Mia had been hoping to leave things on a good note with her mother before the woman abandoned her to Austin, but that hadn't been an option. Truth be told, every conversation with Mom either involved stepping on eggshells or explosives—she never knew which one it would be.

She didn't need Carol Brownstone's approval—she hadn't for years. And yet she spent all of this time being the dutiful daughter, fighting for even a crumb of this woman's affection.

"Well, I'm just going to warn you, women are as difficult as men when it comes to relationships," Mom said as she brought a few more dresses over from her closet. "Both aren't to be trusted with your heart, though it's a shame to hear about Sky. She's such a sweet girl."

Mia couldn't help the laugh that slipped out.

Typical. Out of all of the responses she could've gotten from her mother, that one felt the most on-brand. Who cared about what gender she was attracted to when relationships and falling in love was for suckers? Pure Carol Brownstone.

"What's so funny?" Mom asked, her eyes narrowing as she glanced over. "I'm making sure you don't fill your head full of fancies. You don't want to keep getting hurt like this, do you?"

Mia shook her head. "Nothing's funny, Mom.

Clearly, you've seen my track record with relationships and made the right assessment."

"No need to get smart with me, Mia," Mom said, a slight huff coming from her as she folded another dress.

This woman would never make her feel supported. Her mother might be related to her by blood, but the older she grew, the less she felt like a family.

However, one place in recent memory had been a home.

Whenever Sky was around, Mia found her peace, her warmth, the hearth she'd been seeking. Her chest twisted tight. If only Sky could find the way out of the labyrinth she'd lost herself in, Mia would spend every day by the woman's side and never wander.

One thing had become clear through their time together in the quarantine though—Mia had experienced the depth she'd been searching for all along, and she wouldn't be deceived by shallow, seeking relationships any longer. Even if that meant spending her time finding closer friends or on stopping the impulse to please her mother at every turn. Mia would put those lessons to use, plant those seeds, and water them until they grew into a garden of the relationships she'd been seeking all along.

CHAPTER NINETEEN

Sky sat at the bench, watching the river sparkle under the midday sun.

She'd texted Mia the time and date, knowing the woman's schedule better than her own at this point. Sky had been hoping for a response, but she couldn't fault Mia for not giving one. She swung her feet back and forth, closing her eyes as the sunlight settled onto her skin, the heat permeating through.

With her eyes shut, she could hear the murmur of the river, the scuff of footsteps, and the gentle chatter threading through the air. After so long stuck inside, she treasured every moment she got out and around other people. Over time, the novelty would fade, but right now, she'd bask in every second.

Last night had been her first appointment with the

therapist. No crazy breakdowns or sobbing fits, but the woman spent time trying to get her family history and gave her a packet of homework for the next session. Her calm tone had settled Sky, who had been ready to run screaming in the other direction, from the moment she stepped into the office.

Maybe she could eventually stop thinking of everything as life or death, black and white, past or future.

"What kind of friend invites someone out to take a nap?" Mia's voice sounded in front of her.

Sky's eyes shot open, hungry for a glimpse of the woman. Mia looked damn good, her freckles doubling from time spent in the sun and her gorgeous waves pulled into a low bun. She wore a flowing blue dress that unfurled around her like petals, even as the fabric highlighted her slender waist and devastating curves.

She hadn't realized her heart leapt outside of her body until she saw this woman standing before her.

"Hey, I'm glad you came," Sky murmured, patting the seat next to her. "I wasn't sure if you would, and I couldn't blame you. Not after what an asshole I was."

Mia took a careful seat beside her, inches away. When their eyes met, the desire to close the distance flared there. Sky wanted to kiss her so badly, to ravage her here in the middle of the Riverwalk, damn the onlookers.

Sky chewed on her lip. Right. Showtime. Aubs sent her a reminder this morning, Rehoboth Pact in all caps in case she succumbed to the temptation to chicken out.

She'd been tempted.

"I've been in relationships since Jamie passed, but if I'm being honest, I always kept a part of myself tucked away. If they never knew me—all of me—it'd hurt less when they'd inevitably leave," Sky started. She had to suck in a breath, but when Mia's palm came to rest over hers—well, she'd never needed any more encouragement.

"And then you descended back into my life, the girl I could never have, the one I'd always longed for." All those memories rushed through her, that yearning she'd felt for so many years that the ache had just become a part of her. "At first, it felt too good to be true, and that scared me. But the reason I pulled away, the reason the words always stuck to my tongue was because you understood me, every last thing about me. If we entered into a relationship, well, that would be it for me." Sky's hand in Mia's trembled. "And if you left? I'd lose even more of myself, and after Jamie, a large chunk will always be missing."

Mia squeezed her palm but remained quiet, letting her continue.

Sky looked up to meet the woman's soft blue eyes, as mesmerizing as the river before them. "Mia, I've loved you from the day we became friends in high school, and as I've gotten to know you, I've only loved you more. Some of the happiest memories of my life were the times we spent in my apartment, and Aubs gave me the verbal smackdown I needed. I'd be an idiot to let that go. I'm sorry I didn't speak up when you were leaving."

"You needed time," Mia murmured, her eyes glossing and her voice coming out thick.

"I needed a kick to the ass and therapy—which I've started," she admitted. "But I'm ready to respond now. I want nothing more than to spend forever with you, Mia Brownstone. You've been it for me, from high school on. I've never met a woman more caring, who's willing to bust down my walls when she needs to or speak from her heart even when everyone else is too afraid. You inspire me, every damn day."

"I love you," Mia murmured, a few tears slipping down her cheeks. "I've always loved you, Sky. I just didn't know if you'd ever be ready to take the leap. I know you miss her."

Sky's eyes heated. The reason why Mia never pushed her hard throughout this was because she'd always understood. Sky had locked herself into limbo the moment Jamie died, afraid that if she embraced true joy, true happiness without her sister, that somehow she'd be betraying her memory.

But she'd begun to learn—moving forward didn't mean forgetting the past.

Sky leaned in, wrapping her hands around Mia's cheeks as she pressed a kiss to her lips. The woman was all dark coffee and sweetness, the scent of peaches making her chest ache. She sank into the kiss like the first notes to a favorite melody. In this moment, nothing existed but the gentle thrum of the river, the balmy spring breezes threading around them, and the woman she loved. A pristine, exquisite joy flooded through her.

"You're mine, babe," Sky murmured against Mia's mouth.

"Let's be honest, I always was," Mia responded with a watery grin. "Why meet at the Riverwalk?"

Sky lifted a brow. "Like I wouldn't know your favorite place? You're not as mysterious as you think you are."

Mia ran a thumb along her cheek, a wide grin causing her features to brighten. Like this, she was blindingly gorgeous, so much so that Sky couldn't look at the brilliance for long. "To everyone but you, beautiful."

"I hope you didn't have plans for the rest of the day," Sky murmured. "I have the rare Saturday off and wanted to spend every second with you."

Mia leaned in against her, and Sky wrapped her arm around the woman's shoulders on instinct. Everything about this was as natural as the Delaware River winding through the city before them.

"I missed you," Mia said, her voice steadying. "Every second since I left."

"The apartment hasn't felt the same without you in it," Sky responded. "Though I suppose the living-situation talk can come at a different time."

Mia let out a watery laugh. "We're in no rush. We've got forever, right?" She winked.

Sky's grin widened. "Yeah, forever."

Weeks ago, that would've scared her witless, but as she stared out over the river, glittering under the sunlight, the gentle sway of the water undulating, the truth settled over her.

Sky had been thinking in these finite, big terms that terrified her, when all she'd needed was to take the first step forward.

One day at a time.

"Come on," Mia called from the front door where she'd been waiting for five minutes now, surrounded by luggage.

"I forgot my toothbrush," Sky called from the other room.

"I packed you an extra one," Mia said, leaning against the wall. Out of the two of them, she'd been the more time-oriented one, but she would drag the woman out the door by the ear if this continued. "Hurry, or we'll miss our flight."

Mia glanced at the framed picture hanging beside her. It was the one of Sky, Jamie, and her that she'd sketched and left for Sky. When Sky had moved into Mia's place a few months ago, that was one of the first things they'd put up. Living with Sky felt as natural as it did when they'd been quarantined together, and Mia had realized if she could spend the rest of her life with one person, Sky was it for her.

The little velvet box packed away in her carry-on filled her with fresh sparks every time she thought of it, but she could wait until they arrived in New Orleans. She had plans. After, of course, they traveled to at least one of the restaurants on Sky's extensive must-try list.

Sky rushed up, half breathless, her short brown hair askew, and Mia's impatience melted away.

"Sorry," she said. "I can't tell you the last time I traveled. I keep thinking I'm going to forget something."

"You know what you do then?" Mia said, her voice light. "Go to a pharmacy and grab whatever you forgot. We're just going down South, not Antarctica, love."

"Enough of the sass," Sky said, pressing a quick kiss to her lips. "I thought we needed to get going." Sky's wicked grin pulsed right through her, but they had a hotel room to themselves and plenty of time to explore that once they arrived.

"Bye, Shelley," Mia called out. "Bye, Byron." The cats came rushing up for last-minute scritches, but before Sky could get sidelined again, Mia opened the door and dragged their suitcases out.

Sky took the cue, following her to the car as they began to pack the trunk up the rest of the way. Mia slipped into the driver seat and turned the ignition on, getting ready to race down the highway to the Philly airport. Sky settled into the seat beside her.

"Did you know the original streets of the French Quarter were all named after French royals and nobles?" Sky piped up before Mia even turned the music on.

"About how many more of those gems do you have tucked away?" Mia shot her a look before pulling out of the driveway. Still, a grin rose to her lips. She loved how Sky's mind worked, even when it annoyed her half to oblivion and back. Mia headed down the street, driving toward their destination.

"You probably don't want to know," Sky said, tapping her fingers along the side of the car. "We should find somewhere to have a drink tonight. Celebrate our first trip as a couple."

Little did Sky know, Mia already had a place planned, and it'd be memorable.

"You know," Sky continued. "I've always wanted to go there, but if I'm honest, I'm glad the trip didn't happen until now."

Mia's grin widened, and she reached over with her free hand to squeeze Sky's thigh. "I'm happy I get to experience this with you too. Love you forever and back, beautiful."

Sky tapped the side of her head against the window, a goofy smile on her face. "Love you forever and back too."

Mia merged onto the freeway, pressing hard on the gas pedal. No matter what destination they traveled to or where they went, the moment she'd fallen for Sky, she'd found her home.

***

Looking for more LGBTQI+ romances, check out Katherine's **Midnight Heist**.

ACKNOWLEDGMENTS

This book wouldn't have been possible without my lovely crit partner Catherine Peace, as well as Amy and Stacy for beta reading. Always, always, thank you! I'm also very grateful to my wonderful editors for pushing me to make this manuscript the best it can be. And of course, a huge thanks to Hot Tree Publishing for taking a chance on Mia and Sky's story.

ABOUT THE AUTHOR

Katherine McIntyre is a feisty chick with a big attitude despite her short stature. She writes stories featuring snarky women, ragtag crews, and men with bad attitudes—and there's an equally high chance for a passionate speech thrown into the mix. As an eternal geek and tomboy who's always stepped to her own beat, she's made it her mission to write stories that represent the broad spectrum of people out there, from different cultures and races to all varieties of men and women.

Website: http://www.katherine-mcintyre.com

Newsletter sign-up: http://eepurl.com/duIScb

facebook.com/kmcintyreauthor

twitter.com/pixierants

instagram.com/authorkmcintyre

bookbub.com/profile/katherine-mcintyre

ABOUT THE PUBLISHER

Hot Tree Publishing opened its doors in 2015 with an aspiration to bring quality fiction to the world of readers. With the initial focus on romance and a wide spread of romance subgenres, Hot Tree Publishing has since opened their first imprint, Tangled Tree Publishing, specializing in crime, mystery, suspense, and thriller.

Firmly seated in the industry as a leading editing provider to independent authors and small publishing houses, Hot Tree Publishing is the sister company to Hot Tree Editing, founded in 2012. Having established in-house editing and promotions, plus having a well-respected market presence, Hot Tree Publishing endeavors to be a leader in bringing quality stories to the world of readers.

Interested in discovering more amazing reads brought to you by Hot Tree Publishing? Head over to the website for information:

www.hottreepublishing.com

facebook.com/hottreepublishing
twitter.com/hottreepubs
instagram.com/hottreepublishing

Laura N. Andrews

Lindsay Detwiler

Mary Billiter

Megan Lowe

ML Nystrom

MV Ellis

Natalina Reis

Samatha Harris

Skye McNeil

Theresa Oliver

Virginia Cantrell